THE SAILOR WHO FELL
FROM GRACE WITH THE SEA

Yukio Mishima was born in Tokyo in 1925 into a samurai family. When he graduated from the Peers' School in 1944, he received a citation from the Emperor as the highest honour student. He then attended the Tokyo Imperial University School of Jurisprudence until 1947. Starting in his teens, he became a prolific writer of great diversity, whose works include some fifteen novels (many of which have been made into films), thirty-three plays, two travel books, numerous essays and countless short stories.

Mishima reverenced and mastered the martial arts of Japan. He was a devotee of body-building exercises and also accomplished in the arts of *kendo* and *karate*. He always firmly upheld the traditions of Japan's imperial past – a legacy from his samurai forbears – and believed that these values were being eroded by Western materialism.

On November 25, 1970, at the peak of his brilliant literary career, he astonished the world by committing ritual suicide, or *hara-kiri*, by disembowelment. Mishima had written much about suicide and early death and often expressed the wish to die young. His last work was the tetralogy, *The Sea of Fertility* which is to be published by Penguin in late 1984. This comprises *Spring Snow*, *Runaway Horses*, *The Temple of Dawn* (in two parts) and *The Decay of the Angel* and was finally completed on the morning before his death. Just before his suicide he wrote to friends that he felt empty, having put everything he thought or felt about life into this mammoth undertaking, later hailed as a masterpiece. His writing has been widely acclaimed, compared to that of Proust, Gide and Sartre, and Arthur Miller once said of him that 'He had the economy of means to create enormous myths – his novels are compressed visions.'

YUKIO MISHIMA

The Sailor Who Fell from Grace
with the Sea

Translated from the Japanese by John Nathan

A KING PENGUIN
PUBLISHED BY PENGUIN BOOKS
IN ASSOCIATION WITH
MARTIN SECKER & WARBURG

Penguin Books Ltd, Harmondsworth, Middlesex, England
Penguin Books, 40 West. 23rd Street, New York, New York 10010, U.S.A.
Penguin Books Australia Ltd, Ringwood, Victoria, Australia
Penguin Books Canada Ltd, 2801 John Street, Markham, Ontario, Canada L3R 1B4
Penguin Books (N.Z.) Ltd, 182–190 Wairau Road, Auckland 10, New Zealand

—

Gogo No-Eiko first published in Japan 1963
This translation published in Great Britain by
Martin Secker & Warburg 1966
Published in Penguin Books 1970
Reprinted 1972, 1976 (twice), 1977
Reissued as a King Penguin 1982
Reprinted 1984

—

—

*Lyrics for the song which appears for the first time on page 16,
'I Can't Give Up the Sailor's Life', are from a poem by Ryo Yano*

—

Printed and bound in Great Britain by
Cox & Wyman Ltd, Reading
Set in Intertype Baskerville

Part One *Summer*

Chapter 1

'Sleep well, dear.'

Noboru's mother closed his bedroom door and locked it. What would she do if there were a fire? Let him out first thing – she had promised herself that. But what if the wooden door warped in the heat or paint clogged the keyhole? The window? There was a gravel path below; besides, the second floor of this gangling house was hopelessly high.

It was all his own fault. It would never have happened if he hadn't let the Chief persuade him to sneak out of the house that night. There had been endless questions afterwards, but he hadn't revealed the Chief's name.

They lived at the top of Yado Hill in Yokohama, in a house his father had built. After the war the house had been requisitioned by the Occupation Army and toilets had been installed in each of the upstairs bedrooms: being locked in at night was no great discomfort, but to a thirteen-year-old the humiliation was enormous.

Left alone one morning to watch the house and in need of something to vent his spite on, Noboru began to rummage through his room.

A large chest of drawers was built into the wall adjoining his mother's bedroom. He pulled out all the drawers, and as he was dumping their contents on to the floor he noticed a trickle of light spilling into one of the empty compartments of the chest.

He thrust his head into the space and discovered the source of the light: strong summer sunlight was reflecting off the sea into his mother's empty bedroom. There was plenty of room in the chest. Even a grown-up might squeeze in up to his belly if he lay flat. Peering at his mother's bedroom through the peephole, Noboru sensed something new and fresh about it.

The shiny brass beds his father had ordered from New Orleans were set against the wall on the left side just as they had been before his death. A bedspread was smoothed neatly over one of them, and on the white cloth a large letter 'K' – Kuroda was the family name. A blue straw sun-hat, trailing a long pale-blue ribbon, lay on the bed. On the night-table stood a blue electric fan.

Across the room, near the window, there was a dressing-table fitted with an oval three-piece mirror. The mirror was not quite closed; the upper edges of the glass glinted through the cracks like splinters of ice. In front of the mirror rose a small city of bottles: eau de Cologne, perfume sprays, lavender toilet water, a Bohemian glass goblet, its facets glittering in the light . . . a crumpled pair of brown lace gloves lay withering like cedar leaves.

A couch and two chairs, a floor lamp, and a low, delicate table were arranged directly under the window. An embroidery frame, the beginnings of a pattern needled into the silk, was propped on the couch. The vogue for such things had passed long ago, but his mother loved all kinds of handicraft. The pattern seemed to be the wings of some gaudy bird, a parrot maybe, on a background of silver-grey. A pair of stockings lay in a heap next to the embroidery. The jarring embrace of pure nylon and the imitation damask of the couch gave the room an air of agitation. She must have noticed a ladder on her way out and changed in a hurry.

Only dazzling sky and a few fragments of cloud, hard and glossy as enamel in the light bouncing off the water, could be seen through the window.

Noboru couldn't believe he was looking at his mother's bedroom; it might have belonged to a stranger. But there was no doubt that a woman lived there: femininity trembled in every corner, a faint scent lingered in the air.

Then a strange idea assailed him. Did the peephole just happen to be here, an accident? Or – after the war – when the soldiers' families had been living together in the house . . . He had a sudden feeling that another body, larger than his, a blond, hairy body, had once huddled in this dusty space in the wall. The thought soured the close air and he was sickened. Wriggling backwards out of the chest, he ran to the next room. He would never forget the queer sensation he had when, flinging open the door, he burst in.

Drab and familiar, the room bore no resemblance to the mysterious chamber he had seen through the peephole: it was here that he came to whine and to sulk – *it's time you stopped coming into Mother's room so often with that excuse about wanting to watch the ships; you're not a child any more, dear* – here that his mother would put aside her embroidery to help him with his homework while she stifled yawns, or would scold him for not tying his tie straight, or would check the ledgers she brought home from the shop . . .

He looked for the peephole. It wasn't easy to find. Cunningly hidden in the ornately carved wainscot, in a spot on the upper border where the rippled pattern over-lapped to conceal it – a very small hole.

Noboru stumbled back to his room, gathered the scattered clothing, and stuffed it back into the drawers. When everything was as it had been, he vowed never to do anything that might attract the grown-ups' attention to the chest.

Shortly after he made this discovery, Noboru began spying on his mother at night, particularly when she had nagged or scolded him. The moment his door was closed he would slip the drawer quietly out of the chest, and then watch in unabating wonder while she prepared for bed. On nights when she was gentle, he never looked.

He discovered that it was her habit, though the nights were not yet uncomfortably hot, to sit completely naked for a few minutes before going to bed. He had a terrible time when she went near the wall mirror, for it hung in a corner of the room he couldn't see.

She was only thirty-three and her slender body, shapely from playing tennis every week, was beautiful. Usually she got straight into bed after touching her flesh with perfumed water, but sometimes she would sit at the dressing-table and gaze into the mirror at her profile for minutes at a time, eyes hollow as though ravaged by fever, scented fingers rooted between her thighs. On those nights, mistaking the crimson of her bundled nails for blood, Noboru trembled.

Never had he observed a woman's body so closely. Her shoulders, like the shoreline, sloped gently downwards. Her neck and arms were lightly tanned, but at her chest, as if an inner lamp were burning, began a zone of warm, fleshy white. Her haughty breasts inclined sharply away from her body; and when she kneaded them with her hands, the rosy nipples danced apart. He saw the trembling belly. And the scar that meant she had borne children. A dusty red book in his father's study had taught him that; he had discovered it on the highest shelf, turned the wrong way, sandwiched between a gardening book and a pocket business manual.

And the zone of black. The angle was bad somehow, and he strained until the corners of his eyes began to ache. He tried all the obscenity he knew, but words alone couldn't penetrate that thicket. His friends were probably right when they called it a pitiful little vacant house. He wondered if that had anything to do with the emptiness of his own world.

At thirteen, Noboru was convinced of his own genius (each of the others in the gang felt the same way) and certain that life consisted of a few simple signals and decisions; that death took root at the moment of birth and man's only recourse thereafter was to water and tend it; that propagation was a fiction; consequently, society was a fiction too; that fathers and teachers, by virtue of being fathers and teachers, were guilty of a grievous sin. Therefore, his own father's death, when he was eight, had been a happy incident, something to be proud of.

On moonlit nights his mother would turn out the lights and stand naked in front of the mirror! Then he would lie awake for hours, fretted by visions of emptiness. An ugliness unfurled in the moonlight and soft shadow and suffused the whole world. If I were an amoeba, he thought, with an infinitesimal body, I could defeat ugliness. A man isn't tiny or giant enough to defeat anything.

As he lay in bed, ships' horns often screeched like nightmares through his open window. When his mother had been gentle, he was able to sleep without looking. On those nights, the vision appeared in his dreams instead.

He never cried, not even in his dreams, for hard-heartedness was a point of pride. A large iron anchor withstanding the corrosion of the sea and scornful of the barnacles and oysters that harass the hulls of ships, sinking polished and indifferent through heaps of broken glass, toothless combs, bottle caps and prophylactics into the mud at harbour bottom – that was how he liked to imagine his heart. Some day he would have an anchor tattooed on his chest.

The most ungentle night of all came towards the end of the summer holiday. Suddenly: there was no way of knowing it would happen.

His mother left early in the evening, explaining that she had invited Second Mate Tsukazaki to dinner. To thank him, she said, for having shown Noboru around his ship the day before. She was wearing a kimono of black lace over a crimson under-robe; her obi was white brocade: Noboru thought she looked beautiful as she left the house.

At ten o'clock she returned with Tsukazaki. Noboru let them in and sat in the living-room with the tipsy sailor, listening to stories about the sea. His mother interrupted at ten-thirty, saying it was time for him to go to bed. She hurried Noboru upstairs and locked the bedroom door.

The night was humid, the space inside the chest so stuffy he could scarcely breathe; he crouched just outside, ready to steal into position when the time came, and waited. It was after midnight when he heard stealthy footsteps on the stairs. Glancing up, he saw the doorknob turning eerily in the darkness as someone tried the door;

that had never happened before. When he heard his mother's door open a minute later, he squeezed his sweating body into the chest.

The moonlight, shining in from the south, was reflected back from one pane of the wide-open window. Tsukazaki was leaning against the window-sill; there were gold braid epaulets on his white short-sleeved shirt. His mother's back came into view, crossed the room to the sailor; they embraced in a long kiss. Finally, touching the buttons on his shirt, she said something in a low voice, then turned on the dim floor lamp and moved out of sight. It was in front of the clothes closet, in a corner of the room he couldn't see, that she began to undress. The sharp hiss of the sash unwinding, like a serpent's warning, was followed by a softer, swishing sound as the kimono slipped to the floor. Suddenly the air around the peephole was heavy with the scent of Arpège. She had walked perspiring and a little drunk through the humid night air and her body, as she undressed, exhaled a musky fragrance which Noboru didn't recognize.

The sailor was still at the window, staring straight at Noboru. His sunburned face was featureless except for the eyes that glittered in the lamplight. By comparing him with the lamp, which he had often used as a yardstick, Noboru was able to estimate his height. He was certainly no more than five feet seven, probably a little less. Not such a big man.

Slowly, Tsukazaki unbuttoned his shirt, then slipped easily out of his clothes. Though he must have been nearly the same age as Noboru's mother, his body looked younger and more solid than any landsman's: it might have been cast in the matrix of the sea. His broad shoulders were square as the beams in a temple roof, his

11

chest strained against a thick mat of hair, knotted muscle like twists of sisal hemp bulged all over his body: his flesh looked like a suit of armour that he could cast off at will. Then Noboru gazed in wonder as, ripping up through the thick hair below the belly, the lustrous temple tower soared triumphantly erect.

The hair on his rising and falling chest scattered quivering shadows in the feeble light; his dangerous, glittering gaze never left the woman as she undressed. The reflection of the moonlight in the background traced a ridge of gold across his shoulders and conjured into gold the artery bulging in his neck. It was authentic gold of flesh, gold of moonlight and glistening sweat. His mother was taking a long time to undress. Maybe she was delaying purposely.

Suddenly the full long wail of a ship's horn surged through the open window and flooded the dim room – a cry of boundless, dark, demanding grief; pitch-black and glabrous as a whale's back and burdened with all the passions of the tides, the memory of voyages beyond counting, the joys, the humiliations: the sea was screaming. Full of the glitter and the frenzy of night, the horn thundered in, conveying from the distant offing, from the dead centre of the sea, a thirst for the dark nectar in the little room.

Tsukazaki turned with a sharp twist of his shoulders and looked out towards the water.

It was like being part of a miracle: in that instant everything packed away inside Noboru's breast since the first day of his life was released and consummated. Until the horn sounded, it was only a tentative sketch. The finest materials had been prepared and all was in readiness, verging on the unearthly moment. But one element was lacking: the power needed to transfigure

these motley shreds of reality into a gorgeous palace.
Then, at a signal from the horn, the parts merged into a
perfect whole.

Assembled there were the moon and a feverish wind,
the excited, naked flesh of a man and a woman, sweat,
perfume, the scars of a life at sea, the dim memory of
ports around the world, a cramped breathless peephole, a
young boy's iron heart – but these cards from a gypsy
pack were scattered, prophesying nothing. The universal
order at last achieved, thanks to the sudden, screaming
horn, had revealed an ineluctable circle of life – the cards
had paired: Noboru and mother – mother and man –
man and sea – sea and Noboru . . .

He was choked, wet, ecstatic. Certain he had watched
a tangle of thread unravel to trace a hallowed figure. And
it would have to be protected: for all he knew, he was its
thirteen-year-old creator.

'If this is ever destroyed, it'll mean the end of the
world,' Noboru murmured, barely conscious. *I guess I'd
do anything to stop that, no matter how awful!*

Chapter 2

Surprised, Ryuji Tsukazaki woke up in an unfamiliar
bed. The bed next to his was empty. Little by little, he
recalled what the woman had told him before she had
fallen asleep: Noboru was going swimming with friends
in Kamakura in the morning; she would get up early and
wake the boy, and would come back to the bedroom as
soon as he left . . . would he please wait for her quietly.
He groped for his watch on the night-table and held it up

13

to the light that filtered through the curtains. Ten minutes to eight: probably the boy was still in the house.

He had slept for about four hours, after falling asleep at just the time he would normally be going to bed after night watch. It had been hardly more than a nap, yet his head was clear, the long pleasure of the night still coiled inside him tight as a spring. He stretched and crossed his wrists in front of him. In the light from the window, the hair on his muscled arms appeared to eddy into golden pools; he was satisfied.

Though still early, it was very hot. The curtains hung motionless in front of the open window. Stretching again, Ryuji, with one extended finger, pushed the button on the fan.

Fifteen minutes to Second Officer's watch – stand by please. He had heard the Quartermaster's summons distinctly in a dream. Every day of his life, Ryuji stood watch from noon to four and again from midnight to four in the morning. Stars were his only companions, and the sea.

Aboard the freighter *Rakuyo*, Ryuji was considered unsociable and eccentric. He had never been good at nattering, never enjoyed the gossip supposed to be a sailor's only source of pleasure. Tales of women, anecdotes from ashore, the endless boasting . . . he hated the lowbrow chatter meant to sweeten loneliness, the ritual of affirming ties with the brotherhood of men.

Whereas most men choose to become sailors because they like the sea, Ryuji had been guided by an antipathy to land. The Occupation interdict forbidding Japanese vessels to sail the open sea had been revoked just as he graduated from a merchant-marine high school, and he had shipped out on the first freighter since the war to sail

to Formosa and Hong Kong. Later he had been to India
and eventually to Pakistan.

What a joy the tropics were! Hoping to trade for
nylons or wrist watches, native children met them at
every port with bananas and pineapples and papayas,
bright-coloured birds and baby monkeys. And Ryuji
loved the groves of wine palms mirrored in a muddy,
slow-flowing river. Palms must have been common to his
native land in some earlier life, he thought, or they could
never have bewitched him so.

But as the years passed, he grew indifferent to the lure
of exotic lands. He found himself in the strange predica-
ment all sailors share: essentially he belonged neither to
the land nor to the sea. Possibly a man who hates the
land should never leave it. Alienation and the long
voyages at sea will compel him once again to dream of
life ashore, torment him with the absurdity of longing for
something that he loathes.

Ryuji hated the immobility of the land, the eternally un-
changing surfaces. But a ship was another kind of prison.

At twenty, he had been passionately certain: *there's
just one thing I'm destined for and that's glory; that's
right, glory!* He had no idea what kind of glory he
wanted, or what kind he was suited for. He knew only
that in the depths of the world's darkness was a point of
light which had been provided for him alone and would
draw near some day to irradiate him and no other.

And it seemed increasingly obvious that the world
would have to topple if he was to attain the glory that was
rightfully his. They were consubstantial: glory and the
capsized world. He longed for a storm. But life aboard
ship taught him only the regularity of natural law and
the dynamic stability of the wobbling world. He began to

examine his hopes and dreams one by one, and one by one to efface them as a sailor pencils out the days on the calendar in his cabin.

Sometimes, as he stood watch in the middle of the night, he could feel his glory knifing towards him like a shark from some great distance in the darkly heaping sea, see it almost, aglow like the noctilucae that fire the water, surging in to flood him with light and cast the silhouette of his heroic figure against the brink of man's world. On those nights, standing in the white pilot-house amid a clutter of instruments and bronze signal bells, Ryuji was more convinced than ever:

There must be a special destiny in store for me; a glittering special-order kind no ordinary man would be permitted.

At the same time, he liked popular music. He bought all the new records and learned them by heart while at sea and hummed the tunes when he had a minute, stopping when anyone came near. He liked sea shanties (the rest of the crew scorned them) and his favourite was one called 'I Can't Give Up the Sailor's Life'.

> The whistle wails and streamers tear,
> Our ship slips away from the pier.
> Now the sea's my home, I decided that.
> But even I must shed a tear
> > As I wave, boys, as I wave so sad
> > At the harbour town where my heart was glad.

As soon as the noon watch was over he would shut himself up in his darkening cabin and play the record again and again until it was time for dinner. He always turned the volume down because he didn't want to share the song; besides, he was afraid a fellow officer might drop in with some gossip if he happened to hear the music. The rest of the crew knew how he felt and no one ever disturbed him.

Sometimes, as he listened to the song or hummed it, tears brimmed in his eyes, just as in the lyrics. Strange that a man with no ties should become sentimental about a 'harbour town', but the tears welled directly from a dark, distant, enervated part of himself he had neglected all his life and couldn't command.

The actual sight of land receding into the distance never made him cry. Wharf and docks, cranes and the roofs of warehouses slipping quietly away, he watched with contempt in his eye. Once the casting-off had lit a fire in his breast, but more than ten years at sea had quelled those flames. He had gained only his sunburn and keen eyes.

Ryuji stood watch and slept, woke up, stood watch and slept again. He was full of unexpressed feelings, and his savings steadily increased, for he tried to be alone as much as possible. He became expert at shooting the sun, he counted the stars as friends, he mastered the arts of mooring and warping and towing until finally, listening to the din of waves at night, his ear could discern the surge of the sea from the slake. While he grew more familiar with lustrous tropical clouds and the many-coloured coral seas, the total in his bankbook climbed and now he had almost two million yen* in the bank, an extraordinary sum for a Second Mate.

He had sampled the pleasures of dissipation too. He had lost his virginity on his first cruise. They were in Hong Kong, and a senior officer had taken him to a Chinese whore . . .

*Almost £2,000; one pound = 1,000 yen.

Part One

Ryuji lay on the bed letting the fan scatter his cigarette ash and half closed his eyes as if to weigh in the scales the quantity and quality of the previous night's pleasure against the pitiful sensations of that first experience. Staring into space, he began to see again at the back of his mind the dark wharves of Hong Kong at night, the turbid heaviness of water lapping at the pier, the sampans' feeble lanterns . . .

In the distance, beyond the forest of masts and the lowered straw-mat sails of the moored fleet, the glaring windows and neon signs of Hong Kong outshone the weak lanterns in the foreground and tinted the black water with their colours. Ryuji and the older seaman who was his guide were in a sampan piloted by a middle-aged woman. The oar in the stern whispered through the water as they slipped across the narrow harbour. When they came to the place where the flickering lights were clustered, Ryuji saw the girls' rooms bobbing brightly on the water.

The fleet was moored in three long lines so as to form an inner court of water. All the sterns were facing in and were decorated with sticks of burning incense and red and green paper flags celebrating regional deities. Flowery silk cloth lined the semicircular tarpaulin shells on the flat decks. At the rear of each shell a raised stand, draped with the same material, held a small mirror: an image of Ryuji's sampan wobbled from room to room as they slipped past.

The girls pretended not to notice them. Some lay swaddled in quilts, baring to the cold only dollish, powder-white necks. Others, quilts wrapped around their thighs, played with fortune-telling cards. The luscious reds and golds on the faces of the cards glittered between slender sallow fingers.

'Which one do you want?' the officer asked. 'They're all young.'

Ryuji didn't answer. He was about to choose the first woman in his life and, having travelled sixteen hundred leagues of this bit of dirty, reddish seaweed afloat in the turbid waters of Hong Kong, he felt curiously fatigued, perplexed. But the girls were certainly young, and attractive. He chose before the older man had a chance to offer a suggestion.

The whore had been sitting in silence, her face puckered in the cold, but as Ryuji stepped on to her boat, she laughed happily. And he found himself half-heartedly believing in the happiness he was bringing her. She drew the flowery curtain over the entrance to the shell.

They performed in silence. He trembled a little out of vanity, as when he had first scaled the mast. The woman's lower body, like a hibernating animal half asleep, moved lethargically under the quilts; he sensed the stars of night tilting dangerously at the top of the mast. The stars slanted into the south, swung to the north, wheeled, whirled into the east, and seemed finally to be impaled on the tip of the mast. By the time he realized this was a woman, it was done . . .

There was a knock on the door and Fusako Kuroda came into the room with a large breakfast tray. 'I'm sorry you had to wait so long. Noboru just left a minute ago.' Putting the tray down on the tea table, she opened the curtains and the window. 'There's not a bit of breeze. It's going to be hot again.'

Even the shade beneath the window ledge was as hot as burning asphalt. Ryuji sat up in bed and wrapped the

wrinkled sheet around his waist. Fusako was dressed to go
out. Her bare arms, moving not to embrace him but to
pour morning coffee into cups, seemed unfamiliar. They
were no longer the arms of the night.

Ryuji beckoned Fusako to the bed and kissed her. The
thin, sensitive skin of her lips betrayed the fluttering of
her eyes: this morning, he knew, she was uneasy even
while her eyes were closed.

'What time do you go to work?' he said.

'As long as I can be there by eleven. What are you
going to do?'

'I might go down to the dock for a while, just to see
what's going on.'

They had created in a single night a new situation and
now it appeared to bewilder them. For the moment, their
bewilderment was their only etiquette. Ryuji, with what
he liked to call the unbelievable arrogance of intolerable
people, was calculating how far he might be able to go.

The expression on Fusako's radiant face suggested a
number of things. Resurrection. Or an utter effacement
from memory. Or even determination to prove to herself
and the world that it had not, in any sense of the word,
been a *mistake*.

'Shall we eat over here?' she suggested, moving to the
couch. Ryuji jumped out of bed and threw on his clothes.
Fusako was standing at the window. 'I wish we could see
your ship from here.'

'If that pier wasn't so far out of town . . .' Coming up
behind her, Ryuji put his arms around Fusako's waist.
Together they looked out at the harbour.

The window overlooked the red roofs of old warehouses. A block of new warehouses, like concrete apart-
ment buildings, hulked up from the pier to the north.

The canal was buried under sculls and barges. Beyond the warehouse district piles of seasoning lumber merged into an intricate wooden mosaic. Extending like a concrete finger from the seaward side of the lumber yards, a long breakwater stretched all the way to the sea.

The summer morning sun lay as thin as a dazzling sheet of hammered metal across the colossal anvil of the harbour scene.

Ryuji's fingers touched her nipples through the blue cotton dress. She tossed her head, her hair tickled his nose. As always, he felt as if he had travelled some huge distance, sometimes from the far side of the world, finally to arrive at a point of delicate sensation – a thrilling in his fingertips near a window on a summer morning.

The fragrance of coffee and marmalade filled the room.

'There was something about Noboru this morning, almost as if he knew. Of course, he seems to like you a lot, so it doesn't matter really. . . . I still don't understand how this could have happened. I mean' – her confusion rang a little false – 'it's just incredible!'

Chapter 3

Rex Ltd was one of the oldest and best-known luxury shops in Yokohama's smart Motomachi district. Since her husband's death, Fusako had been running the business by herself. The Moorish architecture of the small two-story building was distinctive; the Mosque window set into the thick white wall at the front of the shop always contained a tasteful display. Inside, an open mezzanine much like a veranda overlooked a patio of imported

Part One

Spanish tile. A small fountain bubbled in the centre of the patio. A bronze Bacchus, some Vivax neckties carelessly draped over its arms, was one of the many curios collected by Fusako's husband before his death; these were priced so as to discourage any would-be buyer.

Fusako employed an elderly manager and four sales-girls. Among the clientele were wealthy foreigners who lived in Yokohama, a large number of dandies and film people from Tokyo, and even some buyers from small retail shops on the Ginza who came down to forage: Rex enjoyed a reputation for uncanny discernment of fine quality, particularly in imported men's wear and accessories. Both Fusako and the manager, a man called Shibuya, who possessed her husband's tastes, were discriminating buyers.

Whenever a ship docked in Yokohama, an import agent who was an old friend of the family used his connexions to get them into the bonded warehouse as soon as the cargo had been unloaded; often Fusako was able to place a bid before other buyers had seen the shipment. Her policy was to emphasize quality labels while providing a wide price range in every item. Rex's order for Jaeger sweaters, for example, would be divided equally between the manufacturer's most exclusive and more modest lines. The same was true of imported Italian leather: Rex's selection included leather from the tanning school attached to the Chiesa Santa Croce in Florence as well as the most expensive gloves and purses from the Via Condotti.

Though Fusako was unable to travel abroad herself, because of Noboru, she had sent Mr Shibuya on a buying trip to Europe the year before, and he had established new connexions all over the Continent. Shibuya had devoted his life to elegance in dress: Rex even stocked

22

English spats, an article not to be found in any of the Ginza shops.

Fusako reached the shop at the usual time and was greeted with the usual morning cordiality. She asked a few business questions and then went up to her office on the mezzanine and opened the day's mail. The air-conditioner in the window whirred solemnly.

Being able to sit at her desk at the usual time was a great relief. It had to be this way. Today of all days, she couldn't imagine what might have happened if she had stayed at home from work.

She took a lady's cigarette from her purse and glanced, as she lit it, at the memo book on her desk. Yoriko Kasuga, a film actress on location in Yokohama, was due to arrive at noon for some colossal shopping; she had just returned from a film festival in Europe and, having spent all her gift money on other things, hoped to cover up with presents from Rex. 'Some stunning French accessories,' she had telephoned to say, 'for about twenty men – pick out whatever you like.' Later in the afternoon, a private secretary from Yokohama Importers was coming over to pick up some of the Italian polo shirts her boss, the company president, wore on the golf links. Faithful customers, these women were remarkably easy to please.

A part of the patio was visible beneath the louvered swinging doors. It was hushed. The tips of leaves on a rubber tree in one corner shone with a dull lustre. Apparently no one had arrived yet.

Fusako was worried that Mr Shibuya might have noticed what felt to her like a flush around her eyes. The old man looked at a woman as though he were examining a piece of fabric in his hand. Even if she was his employer.

She had never actually counted until that morning: five

23

years since her husband's death! It hadn't seemed so long in passing, but all of a sudden, like a white obi she would never be able to wind up, five years was a dizzying length.

Fusako teased the ashtray with her cigarette and then stubbed it out. The man still nested in every nook of her body. She was aware of her flesh beneath the clothes as continuous, thigh and breast in warm accordance: it was a new sensation. And she could still smell the sweat of the man. As if to test them, she curled her stockinged toes.

Fusako had met Ryuji for the first time two days before. Noboru, who was a fanatic about ships, had wheedled her into asking a shipping executive friend for a letter of introduction, and they had gone to see the *Rakuyo*, a ten-thousand-ton freighter anchored at Takashima Pier . . .

Stopping for a minute at the far end of the dock, mother and son had gazed at the cream-and-green-coloured ship gleaming in the distance. Fusako unfurled a parasol with a long white snakeskin handle.

'You see those ships out in the offing?' Noboru said knowingly. 'They're all waiting their turn for a vacant berth.'

'That's why our shipments are always so late getting in,' Fusako drawled. She felt hot just looking up at the ship.

The cloud-dappled sky was partitioned by an intricate criss-cross of hawsers; and lifted towards it in reverence like a slender chin was the *Rakuyo*'s bow, infinitely high, the green banner of the fleet fluttering at its crest. The anchor clung to the hawsehole like a large metal-black crab.

'This is going to be terrific,' Noboru said, brimming

over with boyish excitement. 'I guess we'll be able to look
her over fore and aft.'

'Let's not expect too much, dear, until we're certain
this letter is what we need.'

Thinking about it later, Fusako realized that she had
felt her heart begin to dance even as they had stood looking up at the ship. *That's funny; I'm just as excited as
Noboru.*

The feeling beset her at the height of her languor –
just lifting her head was a hot and wearisome chore – suddenly and for no reason.

'She's a flush deck, Mum – looks a pretty good ship all
right.' Unable to contain the knowledge that crowded his
brain, Noboru held forth to his indifferent mother; as
they drew closer, the *Rakuyo* swelled before them like
great music. Noboru sprinted ahead and raced up the
glittering, silvery gangplank.

But Fusako had to wander down the corridor in front
of the officers' quarters, helplessly clutching her letter to
the Captain. The decks, where unloading was in progress,
were bustling and noisy, but the stuffy corridor was un-
pleasantly hushed.

Then a cabin door marked 'Second Officer' opened
and Tsukazaki appeared.

'Can you tell me where I might find the Captain?'

'He's not here now. Can I help you?'

Fusako showed him the letter; Noboru, eyes shining,
gaped up at the sailor.

'I see – a kind of study trip. I suppose I can show you
round.' His manner was brusque, his gaze never left her
face as he spoke.

That was their first encounter. She would never forget
his eyes as he confronted her in the corridor. Deep-set in

the disgruntled, swarthy face, they sought her out as though she were a tiny spot on the horizon, the first sign of a distant ship. That, at least, was the feeling she had. Eyes viewing an object so near had no business piercing that way, focusing so sharply – without leagues of sea between them, it was unnatural. She wondered if all eyes that endlessly scanned the horizon were that way. Unlooked-for signs of a ship descried – misgivings and delight, wariness and expectation . . . the sighted vessel just barely able to forgive the affront because of the vast reach of sea between them: a ravaging gaze. The sailor's eyes made her shudder.

Tsukazaki took them to the bridge first. The ladder they climbed to the main deck was obliquely runged with bars of summer sunlight. Indicating the freighters anchored offshore, Noboru repeated his knowing observation: 'I suppose all those ships are waiting their turn for a berth –'

'Quite right, sonny. Some of them may have to wait out there four or five days.'

'Do they notify you on the wireless when a berth is vacant?'

'Right again. You get a cable from the company. There's a committee that meets every day to decide berth priorities.'

Sweat was dappling Tsukazaki's white shirt with little spots which revealed the flesh of his powerful back; Fusako was disconcerted. She was grateful to the man for taking Noboru seriously but he made her uncomfortable when he turned to her and asked direct questions. 'The boy knows what he's talking about. Does he want to be a sailor?' His eyes probed her again.

He seemed a rugged, simple man, yet there was also about him an air of indifference and Fusako couldn't determine whether he felt any professional pride. When, opening her parasol against the sun and peering narrowly up at his face, she tried to decide, she thought she discovered something unexpected in the shadow of his heavy brows. Something she had never seen in the broad light of day.

'He'd be wise to forget about it if he is. This is a miserable business if ever there was one,' Tsukazaki said, not bothering to wait for her answer. 'Over here, sonny; this is a mounted sextant.' The instrument he slapped looked like a white mushroom on a long stem.

When they went into the pilot-house, Noboru wanted to touch everything: the speaking tube to the engine room and the automatic-pilot gyro; radar screens; the electronic channel selector. The indicator reading STOP – STAND BY – AHEAD and countless other gauges and dials seemed to summon visions of peril on the open sea. In the chart room next door, he gaped at shelves stacked with maps and tables, and studied an erasure-smudged chart still in the drafting. The chart laced the sea with capricious lines which appeared and reappeared according to some curious un-geometry. Most fascinating of all was the daily log: sunrise and sunset were entered as small semicircles, a pair of golden horns marked the passage of the moon, and the ebb and surge of the tides were shown in gentle, rippling curves.

While Noboru wandered through private dreams Tsukazaki stood at Fusako's side, and the heat of his body in the sultry chart room was beginning to oppress her: when the parasol she had leaned against a desk clattered suddenly to the floor, she felt as if she herself, fainting, had fallen.

She gave a little cry. The parasol had glanced off her

foot. The sailor stooped immediately and picked it up. To Fusako he seemed to move as slowly as a diver under water. He retrieved the parasol and then, from the bottom of this sea of breathless time, his white cap rose slowly towards the surface . . .

Shibuya pushed through the louvered office doors and announced: 'Yoriko Kasuga has just arrived.'

'All right! I'll be right down.'

The old man had recalled her too abruptly; she regretted her tinny, reflex reply.

She studied her face for a minute in a mirror hanging on the wall. She felt as if she were still standing in the chart room.

Yoriko was in the patio with one of her ladies-in-waiting. She was wearing a huge sunflower of a hat.

'I want Mama to do all the choosing. I'm just helpless.'

Fusako objected to being called 'Mama' as though she were the proprietress of a bar. She descended the stairs slowly and walked over to where Yoriko stood chatting.

'And how are you today? It certainly is hot again.' The actress complained about the devastating heat and the crowds at the pier where they were filming. Fusako pictured Ryuji somewhere in the throng and her spirits flagged.

'Thirty cuts this morning – can you imagine that? That's what Mr Honda called "racing through a picture".'

'Will the film be good?'

'Not a chance. But it's not the kind of picture that takes prizes anyway.'

Winning a best-actress award had become an obsession with Yoriko. In fact, the gifts she was buying today constituted one of her inimitable 'gestures' towards the awards jury. Her willingness to believe any scandal (except one involving herself) suggested that she would proffer her body to every member of the jury without hesitation if she thought that might help.

Though she managed with difficulty to support a family of ten, Yoriko was a gullible beauty and, as Fusako well knew, a very lonely woman. Still, except that she was a good customer, Fusako found her almost intolerable.

But today Fusako was enveloped in paralysing gentleness. Yoriko's flaws and her vulgarity were apparent as always, but they seemed as cool and inoffensive as goldfish swimming in a bowl.

'At first I thought sweaters might be nice, since it's almost autumn, but these are supposed to be things you bought this summer, so I picked out some Caldin ties and some polo shirts and a few Jiff pens. For the wives, I don't think you can go wrong with perfume. Shall we go upstairs? I have everything together in the office.'

'I'd love to but I just don't have time. I'll barely have time for a bite of lunch as it is. Can I leave everything to you? The important things are the boxes and wrapping – they're the essence of a gift, don't you think?'

'We'll pack everything beautifully.'

The secretary from Yokohama Importers arrived just as Yoriko was leaving, and she was the last regular customer for the day. Fusako had the sandwich and cup of tea she ordered every day from a coffee shop across the street brought up to her office, and sat down in front of the tray, alone again. Arranging herself comfortably in the chair like a sleeper burrowing under the covers in an attempt to recapture an interrupted dream, she closed her eyes and returned effortlessly to the bridge of the *Rakuyo* . . .

29

Part One

Tsukazaki led them down flights of stairs to the boat deck, whence they could watch cargo being raised from the No. 4 hold. The hatch was a large, dark fissure in the steel plates of the deck at their feet. A man in a yellow steel helmet standing on a narrow ledge just below them was directing the crane with hand signals.

The half-naked bodies of stevedores glistened dully in the dusk at the bottom of the hold. The cargo first took the sun when it was hoisted wobbling up from the bottom high into the mouth of the hatch. Slats of sunlight slipped nimbly over the crates as they wheeled through the air, but faster even than the shattered light the cargo sped, and was hovering above the waiting barge.

The terrifying deliberate prelude and the sudden, reckless flight; the dangerous glitter of silver in a twist of fraying cable – standing under her open parasol, Fusako watched it all. She felt load after heavy load of freight being lifted from her and whisked away on the powerful arm of a crane – suddenly, but after long and careful preparation. She thrilled to the sight of cargo no man could move winging lightly into the sky, and she could have watched for ever. This may have been a fitting destiny for cargo but the marvel was also an indignity. 'It keeps getting emptier and emptier,' she thought. The advance was relentless, yet there was time for hesitation and languor, time so hot and long it made you faint; sluggish, congested time.

She must have spoken then: 'It's been so kind of you to show us round when I know you must be very busy. I was wondering, if you're free tomorrow evening, perhaps we could have dinner together?'

It was a sociable invitation and no doubt Fusako spoke

the words coolly; to Tsukazaki's ear, it sounded like the babbling of a woman stricken with the heat. He looked at her with perfectly honest, puzzled eyes . . .

The night before, they had gone to the New Grand Hotel for dinner. *I was still just trying to thank him then. He ate so properly, just like an officer. That long walk after dinner. He said he'd walk me home, but we got to the new park on the hill and didn't feel like saying good night yet, so we sat down on a park bench. Then we had a long talk. Just rambled on about all kinds of things. I've never talked so much with a man before, not since my husband died . . .*

Chapter 4

After leaving Fusako on her way to work, Ryuji returned briefly to the *Rakuyo* and then took a taxi back through empty, simmering streets to the park where they had stopped the night before. He couldn't think of anywhere else to go until late afternoon, when they had arranged to meet.

It was midday and the park was empty. The drinking fountain was overflowing, dyeing the stone walk a watery black; locusts were shrilling in the cypress trees. The harbour, sprawling towards the sea from the foot of the hill, rumbled thickly. But Ryuji painted out the noontime scene with reminiscences of night.

He relived the evening, paused to savour a moment, traced and traced again the night's course. Not bothering to wipe the sweat from his face, he picked absently at a piece of cigarette paper that clung to his lip while again

31

and again his mind moaned: *how could I have talked so goddam badly!*

He hadn't been able to explain his ideas of glory and death, or the longing and the melancholy pent up in his chest, or the other dark passions choking in the ocean's swell. Whenever he tried to talk about these things, he failed. If there were times when he felt he was worthless, there were others when something like the magnificence of the sunset over Manila Bay sent its radiant fire through him and he knew that he had been chosen to tower above other men. But he hadn't been able to tell the woman about his conviction. He remembered her asking: 'Why haven't you ever married?' And he remembered his simpering answer: 'It's not easy to find a woman who is willing to be a sailor's wife.'

What he had wanted to say was: 'All the other officers have two or three children by now and they read letters from home over and over again, and look at pictures their kids have drawn of houses and the sun and flowers. Those men have thrown their opportunity away – there's no hope for them any more. I've never done much, but I've lived my whole life thinking of myself as the only real man. And if I'm right, then a limpid, lonely horn is going to trumpet through the dawn some day, and a turgid cloud laced with light will sweep down, and the poignant voice of glory will call for me from the distance – and I'll have to jump out of bed and set out alone. That's why I've never married. I've waited, and waited, and here I am past thirty.'

But he hadn't said anything like that; partly because he doubted whether a woman would understand. Nor had he mentioned his concept of ideal love: a man encounters the perfect woman only once in a lifetime and in every case death interposes – an unseen Pandarus – and lures them into the preordained embrace. This fantasy was probably a product of the hyperbole of popular songs. But over the years it had taken on substance in some recess of his mind and merged there with other things: the shrieking of a tidal wave, the ineluctable force of high tide, the avalanching break of surf upon a shoal . . .

And he had been certain that the woman before him was the woman in the dream. If only he had found the words to say it.

In the grand dream Ryuji had treasured secretly for so long, he was a paragon of manliness and she the consummate woman; and from the opposite corners of the earth they came together in a chance encounter, and death wed them. Outdistancing tawdry farewells then, with streamers waving and strains of 'Auld Lang Syne', and far from sailors' fickle loves, they were to descend to the bottom of the heart's great deep where no man has ever been . . .

But he hadn't been able to share even a fragment of his mad dream. Instead he had talked of vegetables: 'Every once in a while when you're on a long cruise and you pass the galley you catch just a glimpse of radish or maybe turnip leaves. And you know, those little splashes of green make you tingle all over. You feel like getting down on your knees and worshipping them.'

'I can imagine. I think I know just how you must feel,' Fusako agreed eagerly. Her voice oozed the joy a woman takes in consoling a man.

Ryuji asked for her fan and shooed the mosquitoes away. Lamps on distant masts twinkled like ochre stars; bulbs in the eaves of the warehouses directly below stretched in regular, bright rows.

Part One

He wanted to talk about the strange passion that catches hold of a man by the scruff of his neck and transports him to a realm beyond the fear of death. But far from finding words for that, he volunteered an account of the hardships he had known, and clucked his tongue.

His father, a civil servant, had raised him and his sister singlehanded after their mother's death; the sickly old man had worked overtime in order to send Ryuji to school; despite everything, Ryuji had grown up into a strong, healthy man; late in the war his home had been destroyed in an air raid and his sister had died of typhus shortly after; he had graduated from the merchant-marine high school and was just starting on his career when his father died too; his only memories of life on shore were of poverty and sickness and death, of endless devastation; by becoming a sailor, he had detached himself from the land for ever. . . . It was the first time he had talked of these things at such length to a woman.

Exaltation swelled Ryuji's voice when he touched on the misery in his life, and while he was recalling the total in his bankbook he couldn't help digressing from the sea's power and benevolence, which was the story he had longed to tell, in order to boast about his own prowess like a very ordinary man indeed. It was just another particular aspect of his vanity.

He wanted to talk about the sea – he might have said something like this: 'It was the sea that made me begin thinking secretly about love more than anything else; you know, a love worth dying for, or a love that consumes you. To a man locked up in a steel ship all the time, the sea is too much like a woman. Things like her lulls and storms, or her caprice, or the beauty of her breast reflecting the setting sun, are all obvious. More than that,

34

you're in a ship that mounts the sea and rides her and yet is constantly denied her. It's the old saying about miles and miles of lovely water and you can't quench your thirst. Nature surrounds a sailor with all these elements so like a woman and yet he is kept as far as a man can be from her warm, living body. That's where the problem begins, right there – I'm sure of it.'

But he could only mouth a few lines of his song: *Now the sea's my home, I decided that. But even I must shed a tear. . . .* 'I guess that's pretty funny. It's my favourite song.'

'I think it's a wonderful song,' she said. But she was only shielding his pride, he knew. Obviously this was the first time she had ever heard the song, though she pretended to know it well. *She can't penetrate to the feelings deep down in a song like this; or see through the murk of my manhood to the longing that sometimes makes me weep; fair enough: then as far as I'm concerned, she's just another body.*

He saw at a glance how delicate and how fragrant a body it was.

Fusako was wearing a black lace kimono over a crimson under-robe, and her obi was white brocade. Her milky face floated coolly in the dusk. Crimson peeped seductively through the black lace. She was a presence suffusing the air around them with the softness of being a woman; an extravagant, elegant woman – Ryuji had never seen anything like her.

The robe shifted fantastically from crimson through shades of purple as every subtle movement of her body altered the play of light from the distant lamps; and he detected within the shadowed folds of cloth the hushed breathing of the woman's own folds. Her sweat and

35

perfumed fragrance reaching him on the breeze seemed to clamour for his death. 'DIE! DIE! DIE!' it screamed; and he imagined the time when her delicate fingertips, stealthy now and reluctant, would quicken into tongues of flame.

Her nose was perfect; her lips exquisite. Like a master placing a *go* stone on the board after long deliberation, he placed the details of her beauty one by one in the misty dark and drew back to savour them.

Her eyes were quiet, and icy, and their chill was lewdness itself, indifference to the world become reckless lechery. Her eyes had haunted Ryuji since they had agreed to meet for dinner the day before; they had kept him awake all night.

And what voluptuous shoulders! Like the shoreline, they began with no real beginning, to slope gently downward from the nape of her neck; gracious, dignified shoulders fashioned so that silk might slip and fall away. *When I hold her breasts they'll nestle against my palms with a marvellous, sweaty heaviness. I feel responsible for all this woman's flesh because it teases me softly like other things that are mine. I'm trembling with the sweetness of her being here, and when she feels me tremble she'll tilt up like a leaf in a wind-tossed tree and show the white backs of those eyes of hers.*

An odd, silly story thrust abruptly into Ryuji's mind. Once the Captain had told him about going to Venice and visiting a beautiful little palace at high tide; and being astounded to find when he got there that the marble floors were under water. . . . Ryuji almost spoke the words aloud: *small beautiful flooded palace.*

'Please talk more,' Fusako begged, and he knew it would be all right to kiss her. The smooth, inflamed play of their lips altered subtly with every contact and clinging

36

release as from angle after angle they poured each other full of light, spinning into a single luminous thread of softness and of sweetness. The shoulders under his rough hands now were more real than any dream.

Like an insect folding in its wings, Fusako lowered her long lashes. Happiness enough to drive a man crazy, Ryuji thought. Happiness that defied description. At first Fusako's breath seemed to climb from somewhere in her chest, but gradually its heat and odour changed until it might have issued from some unfathomable depth within her. Now the fuel firing her breath was different too.

They clutched at each other and collided in frenzied, awkward movements like beasts in a forest lunging at a ring of fire. Fusako's lips softened and became smoother; Ryuji was ready to die happily that very moment. Only when the cool tips of their noses brushed did he realize with a chuckle that they were two firm, separate bodies.

He didn't know how much time passed before, pointing towards a slate roof jutting above the cypress trees at the edge of the park, she said: 'Why don't you stay with us tonight? That's our house over there.'

They stood up and looked around. Ryuji jammed his cap on his head and put his arm around Fusako's shoulders. The park was empty; the red-and-green beacon in the Marine Tower swept across stone benches in the empty square, the drinking fountain, flower beds, and white stone steps.

From habit, Ryuji glanced at his watch. He could just see the dial in the light from the street lamp outside the park: a few minutes past ten. Ordinarily, he would have two hours until night watch . . .

He couldn't take any more of the noonday heat. The

Part One

sun was in the west now, frying the back of his head: he had left his cap on the *Rakuyo*.

The First Mate had given Ryuji a two-day leave, assigning his watch to the Third Mate with the understanding that Ryuji would stand in for him at the next port. He had changed clothes on the ship and had with him a sports jacket and tie he planned to wear that evening, but already sweat had bedraggled his dress shirt.

He looked at his watch. It was only four o'clock. His date with Fusako was for six. The coffee shop where they had arranged to meet had colour television apparently – but there wouldn't be anything interesting on at this hour of the day.

Ryuji walked over to the park railing and looked out at the harbour. The warehouse roofs below were extending their three-corner shadows towards the foreshore. One white sail was tacking back to the yacht basin. He watched the sun sculpture a brace of tensed muscles in marvellous detail in the snow-white blocks of cloud piled above the offing. They were storm clouds all right, but not swollen enough for an evening squall.

The memory of a mischievous game he had often played as a child drew him across the lawn to the drinking fountain. Closing the mouth of the fountain with his thumb, he squirted a fan of water at the dahlias and white chrysanthemums languishing in the heat: leaves quivered, a small rainbow arched, flowers recoiled. Ryuji reversed the pressure of his thumb and doused his hair and face and throat. The water trickled from his throat to his chest and belly, spinning a soft, cooling screen – an indescribable delight.

Ryuji shook himself all over like a dog and, carrying his sports jacket over his arm, moved towards the en-

trance of the park. His shirt was drenched but he didn't
bother to take it off: the sun would dry it quickly enough.

Ryuji left the park. He marvelled at the serenity of the
houses that lined the streets, at the sturdy roofs and
rooted, unbudging fences. As always, the details of shore
life appeared abstract and unreal. Even when he passed
an open kitchen and glimpsed the glitter of polished pots
and pans, everything lacked concreteness. His sexual
desires too, the more so because they were physical,
he apprehended as pure abstraction; lusts which time
had relegated to memory remained only as glistening
essences, like salt crystallized at the surface of a com-
pound. *We'll go to bed together again tonight – this
one's the last: we probably won't sleep at all. I sail tomorrow evening. I wouldn't be surprised if I evaporated
faster than a damned memory, thanks to these two fantastic nights ...*

The heat wasn't making him sleepy. But imagination
whetted his lust as he walked along and he narrowly
avoided a large foreign car that came roaring up the hill.

Then he saw a group of boys break on to the main road
from a footpath near the bottom of the hill. Seeing him,
one of them stopped short – it was Noboru. Ryuji noticed
the boyish kneecaps below the shorts tighten abruptly, saw
tension cramp the face peering up at him; and he recalled
what Fusako had said: *There was something about
Noboru this morning; almost as if he knew. . . .* Battling
with a part of himself that threatened to be flustered in
front of the boy, Ryuji forced a smile and yelled: 'Hey!
Small world, isn't it? Have a good swim?' The boy didn't
answer; his clear, dispassionate gaze was fixed on Ryuji's
shirt.

'Why – how did your shirt get soaked like that?'

Part One

'What, this?' The artificial smile spread over his face again. 'I took a little shower at the fountain up there in the park.'

Chapter 5

Running into Ryuji near the park worried Noboru. He wondered what he could do to keep the sailor from telling his mother about the meeting. In the first place, he hadn't gone swimming at Kamakura as the adults supposed. Besides, one of the boys in the group Ryuji had seen was the Chief. But that wasn't so bad. No one would be able to tell him from the others just by looking – not a chance.

That morning, the boys had left the city with packed lunches and gone all the way to Yamauchi Pier in Kanagawa. For a while they had roamed around the railway siding behind the sheds on the wharf, and then held the usual meeting to discuss the uselessness of Mankind, the insignificance of Life. They liked an insecure meeting place where intrusion was always a possibility.

The Chief, Number One, Number Two, Noboru (who was Number Three), Number Four, and Number Five were all smallish, delicate boys and excellent students. In fact most of their teachers lavished praise on this outstanding group and even held it up as an encouraging example to poorer students.

Number Two had discovered that morning's meeting place and all the others had approved. Behind a large shed marked 'City Maintenance A' a rusty railway siding, apparently in long disuse, crawled through high wild chrysanthemums and old abandoned tyres across an un-

kempt field. Far away in the small garden in front of the
warehouse office, canna flowers were blazing in the sun.
They were dwindling, end-of-summer flames, but so long
as they were visible the boys didn't feel free from the
watchman's eye, so they turned away and followed the
siding back from the shed. The track stopped in front of
a black heavily bolted warehouse door. They discovered
to one side of the warehouse a patch of grass hidden by a
high wall of red and yellow and deep-brown drums, and
sat down. The garish sun was edging towards the summit
of the roof but the little lawn was still in shade.

'That sailor is terrific! He's like a fantastic beast that's
just come out of the sea all dripping wet. Last night I
watched him go to bed with my mother.'

Noboru began an excited account of what he had wit-
nessed the night before. The boys kept their faces blank,
but he could feel every eye on him and the straining to
catch every word, and he was satisfied.

'And that's your hero?' the Chief said when he had
finished. His thin red upper lip had a tendency to curl
when he spoke. 'Don't you realize there is no such thing
as a hero in this world?'

'But he's different. He's really going to do something.'

'Oh? Like what, for instance?'

'I can't say exactly, but it'll be something . . . terrific.'

'Are you kidding? A guy like that never does anything.
He's probably after your old lady's money; that'll be the
punch line. First he'll suck her out of everything she's got
and then, bang, bam, see you around, ma'am – that'll be
the punch line.'

'Well even that's something, isn't it? Something we
couldn't do?'

'Your ideas about people are still pretty naïve,' the

41

thirteen-year-old Chief said coldly. 'No adult is going to be able to do something we couldn't do. There's a huge seal called "impossibility" pasted all over this world. And don't ever forget that we're the only ones who can tear it off once and for all.' Awe-stricken, the others fell silent.

'How about your people?' the Chief asked, turning to Number Two. 'I suppose they still won't buy you an air rifle?'

'Nerp – I guess it's hopeless,' the boy crooned to himself, arms hugging his knees.

'They probably say it would be dangerous, don't they?'

'Yes . . .'

'That's crap!' Dimples dented the Chief's cheeks, white even in summer. 'They don't even know the definition of danger. They think danger means something physical, getting scratched and a little blood running and the newspapers making a big fuss. Well, that hasn't got anything to do with it. Real danger is nothing more than just living. Of course, living is merely the chaos of existence, but more than that it's a crazy mixed-up business of dismantling existence instant by instant to the point where the original chaos is restored, and taking strength from the uncertainty and the fear that chaos brings to re-create existence instant by instant. You won't find another job as dangerous as that. There isn't any fear in existence itself, or any uncertainty, but living creates it. And society is basically meaningless, a Roman mixed bath. And school, school is just society in miniature: that's why we're always being ordered around. A bunch of blind men tell us what to do, tear our unlimited ability to shreds.'

'But how about the sea?' Noboru persisted. 'How

about a ship? Last night I'm sure I caught the meaning of the internal order of life you talked about.'

'I suppose the sea is permissible to a certain extent.' The Chief took a deep breath of the salt breeze blowing in between the sheds. 'As a matter of fact, it's probably more permissible than any of the few other permissible things. I don't know about a ship though. I don't see why a ship is any different from a car.'

'Because you don't understand.'

'Is that right? . . .' An expression of chagrin at this blow to his pride appeared between the Chief's thin, crescent-shaped eyebrows. Their artificial look, as though they were painted on, was the barber's fault: he insisted, despite the Chief's protestations, on shaving his brow and above his eyelids. 'Is that right? Since when is it your place to tell me what I understand and what I don't?'

'C'mon, let's eat.' Number Five was a quiet, gentle boy.

They had just unwrapped their lunches on their laps when Noboru noticed a shadow fall across the lawn and looked up in surprise. The old watchman from the warehouse, his elbows propped on a drum, was peering in at them.

'You boys certainly picked a messy place for a picnic.' With admirable poise, the Chief beamed a scrubbed, schoolboy smile at the old man and said: 'Would it be better for us to go somewhere else? We came down to watch the ships, and then we were looking for a shady place to have lunch . . .'

'Go right ahead; you're not doing any harm. Just be sure not to leave any litter around.'

'Yes, sir.' The smiles were boyish, innocent. 'You don't have to worry about that – we're hungry enough to eat the wrappings and everything; right, you fellows?'

Part One

They watched the hunchback shuffle down the path, treading the border between sunlight and shadow. Number Four was the first to speak: 'There are plenty of that type around – about as common as you can get, and he just loves "the youngsters". I'll bet he felt so generous just now.'

The boys shared the sandwiches and raw vegetables and little cakes in their lunches and drank iced tea from small thermos bottles. A few sparrows flew in over the siding and alighted just outside their circle, but no one shared even a crumb with the birds. Matchless inhumanity was a point of pride with every one of them.

These were children from 'good homes', and their mothers had packed them rich and varied lunches: Noboru was a little ashamed of the plainish sandwiches he had brought. They sat cross-legged on the ground, some in shorts, some in dungarees. The Chief's throat laboured painfully as he wolfed his food.

It was very hot. Now the sun was flaming directly above the warehouse roof, the shallow eaves barely protecting them.

Noboru munched his food in nervous haste, a habit his mother often scolded him for, squinting upwards into the glare as he ate as if to catch the sun in his open mouth. He recalled the painting he had seen the night before. It captured almost perfectly the absolute blue of the night sky. The Chief maintained that there was nothing new to be found anywhere in the world, but Noboru still believed in the adventure lurking in some remote tropical land. And he believed in the many-coloured market at the hub and clamour and confusion in some distant seaport, in the bananas and parrots sold from the glistening arms of black natives.

'You're daydreaming while you eat, aren't you? That's a child's habit.' Noboru didn't answer; he wasn't equal to the scorn in the Chief's voice. Besides, he reasoned, getting mad would only look silly because they were practising 'absolute dispassion'.

Noboru had been trained in such a way that practically nothing sexual, not even that scene the night before, could surprise him. The Chief had taken great pains to ensure that none of the gang would be abashed by such a sight. Somehow he had managed to obtain photographs picturing intercourse in every conceivable position and a remarkable selection of pre-coital techniques, and had explained them all in detail, instructing the boys with some warmth about the insignificance, the unworthiness of such activity.

As a rule a boy with merely a physical edge on his classmates presides at lessons such as these, but the Chief's case was altogether different: he appealed directly to the intellect. To begin with, he maintained that their genitals were for copulating with stars in the Milky Way. Their pubic hair, indigo roots buried deep beneath white skin and a few strands already strong and thickening, would grow out in order to tickle coy stardust when the rape occurred. . . . This kind of hallowed raving enchanted them and they disdained their classmates, foolish, dirty, pitiful boys brimming with curiosity about sex.

'When we've finished eating we'll go over to my place,' the Chief said. 'Everything's all ready for you know what.'

'Got a cat?'

'Not yet, but it won't take long to find one. Nothing will take long.'

Part One

Since the Chief's house was near Noboru's, they had to take another train to get there: the boys liked this sort of unnecessary, troublesome excursion.

The Chief's parents were never at home; his house was always quiet. A solitary boy, he had read at thirteen every book in the house and was always bored. He claimed he could tell what any book was about just by looking at the cover.

There were indications that this hollow house had nourished the Chief's ideas about the overwhelming emptiness of the world. Noboru had never seen so many entrances and exits, so many prim, chilly rooms. The house even made him afraid to go to the bathroom alone: foghorns in the harbour echoed emptily from room to empty room.

Sometimes, ushering the boys into his father's study and sitting down in front of a handsome morocco-leather desk set, the Chief would write out topics for discussion, moving his pen importantly between inkwell and copper-engraved stationery. Whenever he made a mistake, he would crumple the thick imported paper and toss it carelessly away. Once Noboru had asked: 'Won't your old man get mad if you do that?' The Chief had rewarded him with silence and a derisive smile.

But they all loved a large shed in the garden at the back where they could go without passing under the butler's eye. Except for a few logs and some shelves full of tools and empty wine bottles and back issues of foreign magazines, the floor of the shed was bare, and when they sat down on the damp dark earth its coolness passed directly to their buttocks.

After hunting for an hour, they found a stray cat small

46

enough to ride in the palm of Noboru's hand, a mottled, mewing kitten with lacklustre eyes.

By then they were sweating heavily, so they undressed and took turns splashing in a sink in one corner of the shed. While they bathed, the kitten was passed around. Noboru felt the kitten's hot heart pumping against his wet naked chest. It was like having stolen into the shed with some of the dark, joy-flushed essence of bright summer sunlight.

'How are we going to do it?'

'There's a log over there. We can smack it against that – it'll be easy. Go ahead, Number Three.'

At last the test of Noboru's hard, cold heart! Just a minute before, he had taken a cold bath, but he was sweating heavily again. He felt it blow up through his breast like the morning sea breeze: intent to kill. His chest felt like a clothes rack made of hollow metal poles and hung with white shirts drying in the sun. Soon the shirts would be flapping in the wind and then he would be killing, breaking the endless chain of society's loathsome taboos.

Noboru seized the kitten by the neck and stood up. It dangled dumbly from his fingers. He checked himself for pity; like a lighted window seen from an express train, it flickered for an instant in the distance and disappeared. He was relieved.

The Chief always insisted it would take acts such as this to fill the world's great hollows. Though nothing else could do it, he said, murder would fill those gaping caves in much the same way that a crack along its face will fill a mirror. Then they would achieve real power over existence.

Resolved, Noboru swung the kitten high above his head

and slammed it at the log. The warm soft thing hurtled through the air in marvellous flight. But the sensation of down between his fingers lingered.

'It's not dead yet. Do it again,' the Chief ordered.

Scattered through the gloom in the shed, the five naked boys stood rooted, their eyes glittering.

What Noboru lifted between two fingers now was no longer a kitten. A resplendent power was surging through him to the tips of his fingers and he had only to lift the dazzling arc seared into the air by this power and hurl it again and again at the log. He felt like a giant of a man. Just once, at the second impact, the kitten raised a short, gurgling cry . . .

The kitten had bounced off the log for the last time. Its hind legs twitched, traced large lax circles in the dirt floor, and then subsided. The boys were overjoyed at the spattered blood on the log.

As if staring into a deep well, Noboru peered after the kitten as it plummeted down the small hole of death. He sensed in the way he lowered his face to the corpse his own gallant tenderness, tenderness so clinical it was almost kind. Dull red blood oozed from the kitten's nose and mouth, the twisted tongue was clamped against the palate.

'C'mon up close where you can see. I'll take it from here.' Unnoticed, the Chief had put on a pair of rubber gloves that reached up to his elbows; now he bent over the corpse with a pair of gleaming scissors. Shining coolly through the gloom of the shed, the scissors were magnificent in their cold, intellectual dignity: Noboru couldn't imagine a more appropriate weapon for the Chief.

Seizing the kitten by the neck, the Chief pierced the skin at the chest with the point of the blade and scissored a long smooth cut to the throat. Then he pushed the skin to the sides with both hands; the glossy layer of fat beneath was like a peeled spring onion. The skinned neck draped gracefully on the floor, seemed to be wearing a cat mask. The cat was only an exterior; life had posed as a cat.

But beneath the surface was a smooth expressionless interior, a placid, glossy-white inner life in perfect consonance with Noboru and the others; and they could feel their own intricate, soot-black insides bearing down upon and shadowing it like ships moving upon the water. Now, at last, the boys and the cat, or, more accurately, what had been a cat, became perfectly at one.

Gradually the endoderm was bared; its transparent mother-of-pearl loveliness was not at all repellent. They could see through to the ribs now, and watch, beneath the great momentum, the warm, homey pulsing of the colon.

'What do you think? Doesn't it look too naked? I'm not sure that's such a good thing: like it was bad manners or something.' The Chief peeled aside the skin on the trunk with his gloved hands.

'It's naked all right,' said Number Two.

Noboru tried to compare the corpse confronting the world so nakedly with what might have seemed the unsurpassably naked figures of his mother and the sailor; by comparison, they weren't naked enough. They were still swaddled in skin. Even that marvellous horn and the great wide world whose expanse it had limned couldn't possibly have penetrated as deeply as this . . . the pumping of the bared heart placed the peeled kitten in direct and tingling contact with the kernel of the world.

Noboru wondered, pressing a crumpled handkerchief

49

to his nose against the mounting stench, and breathing hotly through his mouth: 'What is beginning here now?'

The kitten bled very little. The Chief tore through the surrounding membrane and exposed the large, red-black liver. Then he unwound the immaculate bowels and reeled them on to the floor. Steam rose and nestled against the rubber gloves. He cut the colon into slices and squeezed out for all the boys to see a broth the colour of lemons. 'This stuff cuts just like flannel.'

Noboru managed, while following his own dreamy thoughts, to pay scrupulous attention to the details. The kitten's dead pupils were purple flecked with white; the gaping mouth was stuffed with congealed blood, the twisted tongue visible between the fangs. As the fat-yellowed scissors cut them, he heard the ribs creak. And he watched intently while the Chief groped in the abdominal cavity, withdrew the small pericardium, and plucked from it the tiny oval heart. When he squeezed the heart between two fingers, the remaining blood gushed on to his rubber gloves, reddening them to the tips of the fingers.

What is really happening here?

Noboru had withstood the ordeal from beginning to end. Now his half-dazed brain envisaged the warmth of the scattered viscera and the pools of blood in the gutted belly, finding wholeness and perfection in the rapture of the dead kitten's large languid soul. The liver, limp beside the corpse, became a soft peninsula, the squashed heart a little sun, the reeled-out bowels a white atoll, and the blood in the belly the tepid waters of a tropical sea. Death had transfigured the kitten into a perfect, autonomous world.

I killed it all by myself – a distant hand reached into

Noboru's dream and awarded him a snow-white certificate of merit – *I can do anything, no matter how awful.*

The Chief peeled off the squeaky rubber gloves and laid one beautiful white hand on Noboru's shoulder. 'You did a good job. I think we can say this has finally made a real man of you – and isn't all this blood a sight for sore eyes!'

Chapter 6

Meeting Ryuji on the way back from the Chief's house just after they had buried the cat was pure bad luck. Noboru had scrubbed his hands, but what if there was blood somewhere else on his body or on his clothes? What if he reeked of dead kitten? What if his eyes betrayed him – like those of a criminal encountering an acquaintance just after the crime?

For one thing, there would be trouble if his mother learned that he had been near the park at this time of day: he was supposed to be in Kamakura with a different group of friends. Noboru had been caught off guard, he was even a little frightened, and he decided arbitrarily that Ryuji was entirely to blame.

The others scattered after hurried good-byes and they were left alone on the hot road with their long afternoon shadows.

Noboru was mortified. He had been waiting for an opening to introduce Ryuji casually. If, under perfect circumstances, the introduction had succeeded, the Chief might have admitted reluctantly that Ryuji was a hero and Noboru's honour would have been redeemed.

51

Part One

But at this unhappy, unexpected meeting, the sailor had presented himself as a pitiful figure in a waterlogged shirt and, as if that wasn't enough, smiled like a fawning idiot. That smile was a disparagement, for it was meant to mollify a child; besides, it transformed Ryuji himself into a disgraceful caricature of the adult lover of youngsters. Overbright and artificial, an unnecessary, outrageous blunder of a smile!

On top of that, Ryuji had said things he should never have said. 'Small world, isn't it? Have a good swim?' And when Noboru challenged the soaking shirt, he should have answered: 'Oh, this? I rescued a woman who had thrown herself off the pier. This makes the third time I've had to go swimming with all my clothes on . . .'

But he hadn't said anything of the kind. Instead he had offered this ridiculous explanation: 'I took a little shower at the fountain up there in the park.' And with that unwarranted smile all over his face!

He wants me to like him. I guess having your new woman's brat like you can be pretty convenient at times.

They found themselves walking in the direction of the house. Ryuji, who still had two hours on his hands, fell into step with the boy, feeling pleased to have found someone to pass the time with. 'There's something funny about both of us today,' he volunteered as they walked along.

Noboru didn't like the show of eager sympathy, but it made asking an important favour easy: 'Mr Tsukazaki, would you mind not telling Mum about seeing me at the park?'

'You bet.'

The sailor's pleasure at being entrusted with a secret, his reassuring smile and quick assent, disappointed Noboru. At least he could have threatened a little.

'I'm supposed to have been at the beach all day – just a minute.' Noboru sprinted to a sand pile at the side of the road and, kicking off his tennis shoes, began to rub his feet and legs with handfuls of sand. The smug, affected boy moved with an animal quickness Ryuji hadn't seen before. Conscious of being watched, Noboru was putting on a show, smearing the sand on the backs of his legs and all the way up his thighs. When he was satisfied, he stepped into his shoes gingerly so as not to dislodge the sand and minced back to Ryuji. 'Look,' he said, indicating the sand on his sweating thigh, 'it stuck in the shape of a draftsman's curve.'

'Where are you heading now?'

'Home. Why don't you come too, Mr Tsukazaki? There's an air-conditioner in the living-room and it's really cool.'

They turned on the air-conditioner and Ryuji slumped into a rattan chair. Noboru, after returning from an artfully reluctant trip to the bathroom under orders from the housekeeper to wash his feet, sprawled on the rattan couch near the closed window.

The housekeeper came in with cool drinks and began to scold again: 'I'm going to tell your mother just how bad you behave in front of company – flopping all over the place like that.'

Noboru's eyes sought help from Ryuji.

'It doesn't bother me a bit. And swimming all day does seem to have tired him out.'

'I suppose so – but he should know better . . .'

Obviously the housekeeper resented Ryuji and she appeared to be venting her disgruntlement on Noboru. Heaving from side to side buttocks heavy with discontent, she lumbered out of the room.

Part One

Ryuji's defence had united them in a tacit pact. Noboru swilled his drink, dribbling yellow fruit juice on his throat. Then he turned to look at the sailor, and, for the first time, his eyes were smiling. 'I know just about everything when it comes to ships.'

'You'd probably put an old pro like me to shame.'

'I don't like to be flattered.' Noboru raised his head from a cushion his mother had embroidered; for an instant, there was fury in his eyes.

'What time do you stand watch, Mr Tsukazaki?'

'From noon to four and from midnight to four. That's why they call it "thieves' watch".'

'Thieves' watch! Gosh, that sounds terrific!' This time Noboru laughed outright and arched his back into a bow.

'How many men stand watch together?'

'A duty officer and two helmsmen.'

'Mr Tsukazaki, how much does a ship list in a squall?'

'Thirty to forty degrees when it gets really bad. Try walking up a forty-degree incline some time. It's like scaling a damn wall – fantastic. There are times when . . .'

Groping for words, Ryuji stared into space. Noboru saw in his eyes the billows of a storm-riled sea and felt mildly seasick. He was ecstatic.

'The *Rakuyo* is a tramp steamer, isn't she, Mr Tsukazaki?'

'Yes, that's right,' Ryuji admitted half-heartedly: his pride was hurt a little.

'I guess most of your routes are between Japan and China and then India, right?'

'You do know what you're talking about, don't you? Sometimes we ship wheat from Australia to England too.'

Noboru's questions were precipitate, his interest leaped

54

from one subject to another. 'What was the Philippines' chief product again?'

'Lauan wood, I guess.'

'How about Malaya?'

'That'd be iron ore. Here's one for you: what's Cuba's chief product?'

'Sugar. What else? Anybody knows that. Say, have you ever been to the West Indies?'

'Yes. Just once, though.'

'Did you get to Haiti?'

'Yes.'

'Boy! How about the trees there?'

'Trees?'

'You know, like shade trees or –'

'Oh, that – palms mostly. And then the mountains are full of what they call flamboyants. And silk trees. I can't remember whether the flamboyant looks like the silk tree or not. Anyway, when they blossom, they look like they're on fire. And when the sky gets pitch black just before an evening storm they turn fantastic colours. I've never seen blossoms like that anywhere else.'

Ryuji wanted to talk about his mysterious attachment to a grove of wine palms. But he didn't know how to tell that kind of story to a child, and as he sat and wondered, the doomsday glow of sunset in the Persian Gulf awoke in his mind, and the sea wind caressing his cheek as he stood at the anchor davit, and the rankling fall of the barometer that warned of an approaching typhoon: he was sensible again of the sea's nightmarish power working endlessly on his moods, his passions.

Noboru, just as he had seen storm billows a minute before, beheld one by one in the sailor's eyes the phantoms he had summoned. Surrounded by visions of distant lands and by white-paint nautical jargon, he was being swept away to the Gulf of Mexico, the Indian Ocean, the Persian Gulf. And the journey was made possible by this authentic Second Mate. Here at last was the medium without which his imagination had been helpless. How long he had waited for it!

Rapturously, Noboru shut his eyes tight.

The two-horsepower motor in the air-conditioner whispered to the room. It was perfectly cool now, and Ryuji's shirt had dried. He clasped his rough hands behind his head: the ridges in the finely laced rattan nestled coolly against his fingers.

His eyes roved the dim room and he marvelled at the golden clock enthroned on the mantelpiece, the cut-glass chandelier hanging from the ceiling, the graceful jade vases poised precariously on open shelves: all delicate, all absolutely still. He wondered what subtle providence kept the room from rocking. Until a day before, the objects here had meant nothing to him, and in a day he would be gone; yet, for the moment, they were connected. The link was a glance met by a woman's eyes, a signal emanating from deep in the flesh, the brute power of his own manhood; and to know this filled him with a sense of mystery, as when he sighted an unknown vessel on the open sea. Though his own flesh had fashioned the bond, its enormous unreality with respect to this room made him tremble.

What am I supposed to be doing here on a summer afternoon? Who am I, sitting in a daze next to the son of a woman I made last night? Until yesterday I had my song – 'the sea's my home, I decided that' – and the tears I cried for it, and two million yen in my bank account as guarantees of my reality – what have I got now?

Noboru didn't realize that Ryuji was sinking into a void. He didn't even notice that the sailor wasn't looking in his direction any more. Lack of sleep and a succession of shocks had exhausted him, the bloodshot eyes he had told the housekeeper were from the salt water were beginning to close. He pondered, as he rocked towards sleep, the glistening figures of absolute reality twice glimpsed since the night before during lapses in the unmoving, tedious, barren world . . .

He saw them as marvellous gold embroideries leaping off a flat black fabric: the naked sailor twisting in the moonlight to confront a horn – the kitten's death mask, grave and fang-bared – its ruby heart . . . gorgeous entities all and absolutely authentic: then Ryuji too was an authentic hero . . . all incidents on the sea, in the sea, under the sea – Noboru felt himself drowning in sleep. 'Happiness,' he thought. 'Happiness that defies description . . .' He fell asleep.

Ryuji looked at his watch: it was time to go. He knocked lightly on the door leading to the kitchen and called the housekeeper.

'He's fallen asleep.'

'That's just like that boy.'

'He might catch a chill. If there's a blanket or something –'

'I'll get one from upstairs.'

'Well – I'll be going now.'

'I suppose we can expect you back tonight?' A smirk appeared around the housekeeper's eyes and trickled down her face as she glanced once, quickly, ogling up at Ryuji.

Chapter 7

Since dark antiquity the words have been spoken by
women of every caste to sailors in every port; words of
docile acceptance of the horizon's authority, of reckless
homage to that mysterious azure boundary; words never
failing to bestow on even the haughtiest woman the sadness, the hollow hopes, and the freedom of the whore:
'You'll be leaving in the morning, won't you?...'

But Fusako was determined not to submit, though she
knew Ryuji would try to make her speak. She understood
that he was staking a simple man's pride on the tears of a
woman lamenting the farewell. And what a simple man
he was! Their conversation in the park the night before was proof of that. First he had misled her with his
pensive look into expecting profound observations or
even a passionate declaration, and then he had begun a
monologue on shreds of green leaf, and prattled about
his personal history, and finally, horribly entangled
in his own story, burst into the refrain of a popular
song!

Yet she was relieved to know that he was not a dreamer,
and his plainness, a quality more durable than imagina-
tive, like a piece of sturdy old furniture, she found reassuring. Fusako needed a guarantee of safety, for she
had pampered herself too long, avoided danger in any
form, and her unexpected and dangerous actions since
the night before had frightened her. Feeling up in the air
as she did, it seemed vitally important that the man with
whom she was involved be down-to-earth. There were
still things to learn of course, but at least she was con-

vinced that Ryuji was not the sort of man to burden her financially.

On their way to a steakhouse at the Bashado, they passed a little café with a fountain in the garden and small red and yellow lights strung along the awning over the entrance, and decided to go in for a drink before dinner.

For some reason, the mint frappé Fusako ordered was garnished with a cherry, stem and all. She deftly tore the fruit away with her teeth and placed the stone in a shallow glass ashtray.

The glow that lingered in the sky was sifting through the lace curtains on the large front window, suffusing the almost empty room. It must have been due to those delicately tinted rays of light: the smooth, warm cherry stone, just perceptibly beginning to dry and ineffably pink, appeared incredibly seductive to Ryuji. He reached for it abruptly and put it into his mouth. A cry of surprise rose to Fusako's lips, then she began to laugh. She had never known a moment of such peaceful physical intimacy.

They chose a quiet neighbourhood for a walk after dinner. Captives of a tenderness that might have bewitched the summer night, they walked in silence, holding hands. Fusako brushed at her hair with her free hand. That afternoon she had watched for a lull in business at the shop, then dashed to the beauty parlour for a quick hairdo. Remembering the puzzlement on the beautician's face when she had declined the perfumed oil which she always got her to comb lightly through her hair, Fusako blushed. Now her whole body threatened to unravel into a sloppy heap amid the smells of the city and the summer night.

Part One

Tomorrow, the thick fingers twined in her own would plunge over the horizon. It was unbelievable, like a ridiculous, spectacular lie. Fusako blurted out, as they were passing a nursery that had closed for the day: 'I've sunk pretty low, thanks to you.'

'Why?' Surprised, Ryuji stopped.

Fusako peered through the wire fence at the trees and shrubbery and rose bushes all tightly packed together in the nursery garden. It was pitch dark, the luxuriant foliage was unnaturally tangled and involuted: she felt suddenly as though a terrible eye were looking into her.

'Why?' Ryuji asked again; Fusako didn't answer. As the mistress of a respectable shore household, she wanted to protest at being forced into a pattern of life which began with waving goodbye to a man, a pattern familiar to any harbour whore. But that would have been only one step away from giving utterance to those other words: You'll be leaving in the morning, won't you? . . .

A solitary life aboard ship had taught Ryuji not to probe matters he didn't understand. Fusako's complaint he interpreted as typical, a woman whining; his second 'why' was therefore playful, teasing. The thought of parting with her the next day was painful, but he had a maxim to countermand his pain, an insubstantial refrain which played over and over in his dreams: 'The man sets out in quest of the Grand Cause; the woman is left behind.' Yet Ryuji knew better than anyone that no Grand Cause was to be found at sea. At sea were only watches linking night and day, prosaic tedium, the wretched circumstances of a prisoner.

And the admonishing cables: 'Recently vessels of this line have been plagued by a succession of collisions in the Irako Channel and at the northern entrance to

Kijima Straits stop request extreme caution in narrow channels and harbour entrances stop in view of this line's current situation request redoubled efforts to eliminate all accidents at sea stop Director of Maritime Shipping.' The cliché 'in view of this line's current situation' had been included in every wordy cable since the beginning of the so-called shipping slump.

And the Quartermaster's log, a daily record of weather, wind velocity, atmospheric pressure, temperature, relative humidity, speed, distance logged, and revolutions per minute, a diary accurately recording the sea's caprice in compensation for man's inability to chart his own moods.

And, in the mess room, traditional dancing dolls, five portholes, a map of the world on the wall. The soy-sauce bottle was suspended from the ceiling on a leather strap; sometimes round bars of sunlight lanced towards the bottle and slipped back, darted in again as if to lap the lurching, tea-brown liquid, then withdrew again. Posted on the galley wall was an ostentatiously lettered breakfast menu:

> Miso Soup with Eggplant and Bean Curd
> Stewed White Radishes
> Raw Onions, Mustard, Rice

Lunch was Western style and always began with soup.

And the green engine, tossing and moaning inside its twisted tubes like the feverish victim of a fatal disease . . .

In a day, all this would become Ryuji's world again.

They had stopped in front of a small gate in the nursery fence. Ryuji's shoulder brushed against the gate and it clicked open, swinging in towards the garden.

'Look, we can go inside.' Fusako's eyes were sparkling like a child's.

Part One

With a furtive eye on the lighted window in the watchman's shack, they stole into the dense, man-made forest; there was scarcely room to step. They clasped hands and made their way through the shoulder-high thicket, pushing thorny rose stems aside and stepping over flowers at their feet until they emerged in a corner of the garden occupied by tropical trees and plants, a lush tangle of orchids and banana trees, rubber trees and all varieties of palm.

Seeing Fusako here in her white suit, Ryuji felt that their first meeting must have been in some tropical jungle. Deliberately, cautious of pointed leaves at eye level, they moved together and embraced. The fragrance of her perfume rose above the low droning of mosquitoes; Ryuji was anguished, unaware of time and place.

Outside, only a slender wire fence away, small neon lights were twinkling like goldfish; every few minutes the headlights of a passing car mowed down the shadows of their forest. The glow of a red neon sign flashing across the street carried to Fusako's palm-shadowed face, brought a delicate blush to her white cheeks and blackened her red lips. Ryuji kissed her.

The long kiss plunged them into private pools of sensation. Fusako was aware only of the next day's parting. Stroking Ryuji's cheek, touching the hot, lacquered surfaces where he had shaved, smelling the odour of flesh rising from his agitated chest, she sensed every nerve in his body screaming goodbye. His tight, furious embrace told her how desperately he wanted to affirm that she was real and really with him.

For Ryuji the kiss was death, the very death in love he always dreamed of. The softness of her lips, her mouth so crimson in the darkness he could see it with closed eyes, so infinitely moist, a tepid coral sea, her restless tongue quivering like sea grass . . . in the dark rapture of all this was something directly linked to death. He was perfectly aware that he would leave her in a day, yet he was ready to die happily for her sake. Death roused inside him, stirred.

Then the pale tremor of a ship's siren floated in from the direction of Centre Pier and settled over the garden. A nebulous mist of sound, it would never have registered on Ryuji's ear if he hadn't been a sailor. *Funny time of night for a freighter to be pulling out — I wonder how they got her loaded so fast.* The thought broke the spell of the kiss; he opened his eyes. And he could feel the siren probing deep inside him, rousing his passion for the Grand Cause. But what was it? Maybe another name for the tropical sun.

Ryuji drew away from Fusako's lips and began fumbling in his vest pocket. She waited. There was a harsh rustling of paper and he produced a crooked cigarette and placed it between his lips; but Fusako angrily snatched the lighter out of his hand. He leaned towards her. 'Don't expect me to give you a light, because I won't.' The lighter flared with a metallic click, the flame danced in her unmoving eyes as she held it to a hemp leaf. The withered tassels should have fired quickly but the flame wouldn't catch. Her engrossment, the steadiness of her hand, made Ryuji afraid.

Then the little flame lit up her cheek and he saw the string of tears. Fusako put out the lighter when she realized he had noticed. Ryuji embraced her again and, relieved by the assurance of her tears, he began to cry too.

Noboru waited irritably for his mother to come home.

Part One

At ten o'clock he heard the telephone ring. A minute later the housekeeper came to his room with a message.

'Your mother just called to say she's going to stay the night at a friend's. She'll be back in the morning to change before she goes to the shop; and you're to spend the evening catching up on all that summer homework.'

Never before, not as far back as he could remember, had his mother ever stayed out all night. The development itself was no surprise, but he flushed with rage and apprehension. He had been looking forward all day to the peephole: there was no telling what revelations, what miracles it might have disclosed again tonight. He wasn't at all sleepy, on account of the nap he had taken in the afternoon.

The desk was covered with holiday tasks he had to finish before the new term began; there were only a few days left. But Ryuji was leaving the next day and then his mother would help him again. Or would she just wander around in a daze, too preoccupied to worry about her own son's homework? Not that it made much difference: Japanese and English and art were the only subjects she could handle. She was never much help with social studies, and he knew more about maths and science than she did. How could anyone that bad at maths run a business? She was probably always at Mr Shibuya's mercy.

Noboru opened a textbook and skimmed a few pages but he couldn't concentrate. He was too disturbed by the indisputable fact that Ryuji and his mother were not in the house.

He stood up, sat down, and at last began to pace the small room. What could he do to get to sleep? Go into his mother's room and watch the mast lamps in the harbour?

The red lamps on some of the ships blinked on and off all night; there might even be a freighter sailing again, and another screaming siren.

Then he heard the door to the next room open. Maybe his mother had been trying to fool him and had come home with Ryuji after all. He slipped the drawer quietly out of the dresser and lowered it to the floor. He was already dripping wet.

This time there was a knock at his own door! He couldn't let anyone see the drawer sitting in the middle of the floor at this time of night; he scrambled to the door and pushed against it with all his might. The doorknob rattled harshly.

'What's going on in there? Can't I come in?' But it was the housekeeper's voice. 'Are you all right? Go ahead and be stubborn then; but you'd better turn those lights out and get to bed – it's almost eleven.'

Noboru was still leaning against the door, maintaining an obstinate silence, when a key was rammed into the lock and roughly turned. He was aghast. It had never occurred to him that the housekeeper might have a key; he had assumed that his mother had taken all the keys with her when she went out.

Furious, his brow dripping sweat, he wrenched the doorknob with all his strength; the door didn't open. The housekeeper's footsteps faded as she descended the groaning stairs.

Noboru had hoped to take advantage of this one-in-a thousand chance by sneaking over to the Chief's house and waking him with a password whispered outside his window. Now this last, fervent hope was dashed to bits. He despised all mankind. And he wrote a long entry in his diary, not forgetting to set down Ryuji's crimes.

Part One

CHARGES AGAINST RYUJI TSUKAZAKI

ONE: *smiling at me in a cowardly, ingratiating way when I met him this morning.*

TWO: *wearing a dripping-wet shirt and explaining that he had taken a shower in the fountain at the park – just like an old bum.*

THREE: *deciding arbitrarily to spend the night out with Mother, thereby placing me in a dreadfully isolated position.*

But after thinking it over, Noboru erased the third count. It was obviously a contradiction of the first two, which were aesthetic, idealistic, and therefore objective value judgements. The subjective problem in the third charge was only proof of his own immaturity, not to be construed as a crime on Ryuji's part.

Noboru squeezed a mountain of toothpaste on to his toothbrush and belaboured his mouth until the gums bled. Staring into the mirror, he watched a pistachio foam swaddle his irregular teeth until only the shiny pointed edges of the boyish cuspids showed; he was despondent. The smell of peppermint made a purity of his rage.

Tearing off his shirt, Noboru put on his pyjama tops and looked around the room. As if it were material evidence, the dresser drawer was still on exhibit in the middle of the floor. He lifted it, surprised by a heaviness he hadn't noticed before, and was about to return it to the chest when he changed his mind and put it down again. He slipped into the space in the wall with practised ease.

The hole had been closed, he thought for one terrifying instant; then, groping with his fingers, he discovered that it was open as before. There simply wasn't enough light on the other side to reveal it at a glance.

Noboru pressed his eye to the peephole. When the door

had opened before, he realized, it had been the house-keeper going in to draw all the curtains. Gradually the pupil strained open, and he discerned around the brass bedsteads a glimmer of light, a wisp of brightness hardly more than a trace of mould.

The room as a whole, feverish with vestiges of the noon heat, was as black as the inside of a large coffin, everywhere a shade of darkness, and alive with jostling particles of something Noboru had never seen, the blackest thing in all the world.

Chapter 8

They spent the night in a small old hotel not far from the docks: Fusako was afraid she might be recognized at one of the large downtown hotels. She had often passed this drab, two-storey building but had never imagined as she glanced through the glass doors at the entrance and saw the dim, outsize lobby, the scarred front desk, and the large steamship calendar bedizening one calcimined wall, that she would be staying here one day.

They slept for a few hours in the early morning, then separated until sailing time. Fusako went home to change clothes before going to work, Ryuji returned to the pier. He had to stand in for the First Mate, who was going ashore to do some shopping. He would have been busy in any case because the maintenance of ropes and other tackle so important in the loading operation was one of his regular duties.

The *Rakuyo* was due to sail at six; and thanks to four days and nights of perfect weather, loading had proceeded on schedule. The freighter was bound for Santos, her meandering course to be determined by consignors in ports along the way.

Fusako came home at three, changed into a cotton *yukata* so that Ryuji might have a last look at a woman in a kimono, and left for the pier with Noboru. Traffic was light: it was only a few minutes after four when they arrived. A few trucks and a crane were still clustered round one of the concrete sheds, the boom on the *Rakuyo*'s foredeck still wobbled between her hatches and the pier. Fusako decided to wait in the air-conditioned car until Ryuji came down to meet them.

But Noboru couldn't sit still. He bolted out of the car and raced up and down the bustling pier, inspecting the barges moored below and exploring unlocked sheds.

Inside the largest, reaching almost to the crisscross of green steel beams at the ceiling, were stacks of new white wooden crates with black metal clasps at the corners and words stamped in English on the side slats. Noboru, as he watched a siding fade to nothing amid the towering freight, felt a thrill of joy at having come to the end of the dream that railways wake in children, and also mild disappointment: it was like tracing the course of a familiar river and discovering its tiny source.

'Mum! Hey, Mum!' Racing back to the car, Noboru drummed on the window: he had spotted Ryuji standing near the windlass in the ship's bow.

Fusako got out of the car and they waved at the high distant figure in a dirty khaki shirt. Ryuji raised one hand in reply, then moved busily out of sight. Noboru thought of the sailor toiling now, and soon to sail away; and he was flushed with pride.

Fusako could only wait for Ryuji to appear again. Un-furling a parasol with a silver handle, she watched the

Rakuyo's swaying hawsers cut thick gashes across the harbour's face. The dock was broiling under the western sun,
washed with light and dazzling to the eye; and eating into
all the steel and concrete, like the salt in a sea wind, was
a strong, smarting grief. The same grief was diffused
through the bright air, its force imparting to the occa-
sional clatter of deck plates and the crash of hurled cables
a long, hollow reverberation.

The concrete pier trapped the heat and hurled it back
as a scorching glare; the light breeze blowing off the water
brought no relief.

They squatted at the edge of the sea-wall with their
backs to the ferocious sun, and stared at the wavelets
mincing in to break and foam against the white-flecked
stone. Rocking slightly like a rough-hewn cradle, one of
the barges moored below edged towards the wall, then
slipped back while another sidled in. A seagull skimmed
over the wash that flapped on the open decks; a shiny
log floating amid other garbage on the dirty water rode
round and round on the eddying swell. The waves ad-
vanced in tiers, flank blending subtly with azure flank
until it seemed that this endlessly repeated pattern was all
they could see as they gazed at the water.

Noboru read off the draught numbers painted on the
Rakuyo's side; 60 was just above the water, 84 and 86
bracketed the water line, 90 was almost as high as the
hawsehole.

'Do you think the water ever gets that high? Gosh, it
must be quite something if it does.'

Noboru had guessed his mother's mood and she was
reminding him as she stared out to sea of that lonely,
naked figure in front of the mirror; the question was as
boyish as he could make it, but Fusako didn't answer.

Part One

Across the harbour basin, pale grey smoke hovered above the streets of Naka Ward; the red-and-white-striped beacon tower aspired to clearer sky. The middle distance was a dense forest of white masts and, still farther out, a bank of clouds luminous in the late afternoon sunlight heaped and twisted above the water.

A steam launch towing an unloaded barge pulled away from the far side of the *Rakuyo* and chugged out of sight.

It was just after five when Ryuji came off the ship. The silver chains which would raise the gangplank had already been attached. A gang of longshoremen wearing yellow helmets had filed down the gangplank, piled into a Longshoremen's Union bus, and left the pier. The eight-ton Port Authority derrick had gone, the hatches had been bolted down. Then, finally, Ryuji appeared.

Noboru and Fusako chased long shadows towards the sailor. Ryuji squashed Noboru's straw hat with the palm of his hand and laughed as the boy struggled to pull the brim up over his eyes. The work had exhilarated him.

'We'll be leaving any minute now. I'll be aft when we cast off.' Ryuji gestured towards the distant stern.

'I decided to wear a kimono. You won't be seeing any for quite a while now –'

'I guess not – except maybe on old *nisei* ladies travelling with American tours.'

They found surprisingly little to say. Fusako considered mentioning how lonely she was going to be and decided not to. The parting, like the white fruit of an apple discolouring instantly around the bite, had begun three days before when they had met aboard the *Rakuyo*. Saying good-bye now entailed not a single new emotion.

Noboru, as he affected childishness, was standing guard

over the perfection of the adults, of the moment. His was the sentinel's role. The less time they had, the better. The shorter this meeting was, the less perfection would be marred. For the moment, as a man leaving a woman behind to voyage around the world, as a sailor, and as a Second Mate, Ryuji was perfect. So was his mother. As a woman to be left behind, as a beautiful sailcloth full-blown with happy memories and the grief of parting, she was perfect too. Both had blundered dangerously during the past two days but at the moment their behaviour was beyond reproach. If only Ryuji didn't say something ridiculous and spoil it all before he was safely under way. Peering from beneath the broad brim of his straw hat, Noboru anxiously studied first one face and then the other.

Ryuji wanted to kiss Fusako but he was intimidated by Noboru. Besides, like a man who knows he is dying, he felt a need to be equally tender to all. At the moment, the memories and feelings of others seemed far more important than his own; yet somewhere beneath the sweet agony of self-denial was a desire to get away as quickly as possible.

Fusako still couldn't permit herself to imagine the anxious, exhausting wait to come. She devoured the man with her eyes, testing the sufficiency of that bond. But how self-contained he looked, like a refractory object not even attempting to extend itself beyond its contours. She wished he could be something less defined, like mist. This horrid hulk was too much like rock to fade from memory: the heavy brows, for example, or the too solid shoulders . . .

'Don't forget to write – and use all different kinds of stamps,' Noboru said, perfectly in command of his role.

'You bet. I'll send something from every port. And you

write too. A sailor looks forward to letters more than anything.'

He explained that he had to go aboard to help with the final preparations. They all shook hands. Ryuji climbed the silvery gangplank, turned at the top, and waved his cap.

The sun was just above the warehouse roofs, setting fire to the western sky and searing shadow images of king posts and mushroom ventilators into the dazzling white steel of the bridge. Noboru watched the seagulls wheeling overhead; their wings were dark, their bellies, when they breasted the light, turned yellow as yolks.

Trucks and cranes and dollies had withdrawn from the *Rakuyo* and the dock was empty and still, awash with light. A deckhand dwarfed by distance was still scrubbing a high railing on the *Rakuyo*'s deck and another, a patch over one eye and a paint can in his hand, painting what might have been a window frame. Noboru hadn't noticed the blue and white and red signal flags being hoisted up the mast; at the top of the spire, the Blue Peter fluttered. They walked slowly towards the stern.

All the louvered, dark-green warehouse doors were lowered; large 'No Smoking' signs and the names of major ports scrawled in chalk – Singapore, Hong Kong, Lagos – covered the dismal stretch of wall. Tyres and rubbish bins and the dollies parked in neat rows cast their long shadows across the concrete pier.

The stern high above them was still deserted. There was a quiet sound of water draining, a Japanese flag flapped in the shadow of the anchor davit.

The first stridulous blast of the siren came at fifteen minutes to six. Noboru, listening, knew that the phantom he had watched two nights before was real, understood that he was present at the spot where all dreams began and ended. Then he saw Ryuji; he was standing next to the Japanese flag.

'He might hear you if you yell loud enough,' Fusako urged. The shout left his throat just as the siren subsided; he was horrified by the shrillness of his voice. Ryuji peered down at them and waved; he was too far away to see the expression on his face. Then he turned back to his work with the same twist of his shoulders that had turned him to face the moonlit siren, and didn't look their way again.

Fusako glanced towards the prow. The gangplank had been raised; the last link between ship and shore was broken. The *Rakuyo*'s green-and-cream-coloured side looked like the blade of a colossal axe fallen out of the heavens to cleave the shore asunder.

Smoke began to pour from the funnels. Pitch black, it billowed into the sky in huge clouds which rose to smudge the pale zenith.

'Stand by, fore-station – make ready to weigh anchor.'

'Take up on that slack!' There was another short blast on the siren.

'That's good, fore-station.'

'Right.'

'Weigh anchor – head line away – shore lines away!'

The *Rakuyo* inched away from the pier as the tugboat toiled into the harbour with the stern in tow. The breadth of water sparkling between the ships and the sea-wall fanned open, and even as their eyes were pursuing the receding glitter of the gold braid on Ryuji's cap, the ship had pivoted a full ninety degrees and was at right angles to the pier.

The *Rakuyo* was transformed into an illusory phantom as angles altered from one instant to the next. Gradually,

73

as the stern was towed farther out into the harbour, the long ship folded like a panelled screen while the superstructure on deck overlapped, piled into impacted tiers, and, trapping sunlight in every pocket and dent, soared skyward like a shining pagoda of steel. But the effect was only momentary. Now the tug began to circle back in order to face the bow towards open sea, and the storied tower thrusting up from the deck was dismantled; each object in succession from bow to stern resumed its proper shape until finally the stern itself reappeared and a matchstick figure just recognizable as Ryuji swung back into the splendour of the setting sun.

'Tow lines away –' The voice on the loudspeaker was still clear when it reached them on the wind. The tug pulled away.

Poised motionless on the water, the ship sounded three blasts on her horn. Uneasy silence followed, an interval of quiescence during which it seemed that Ryuji aboard ship and Fusako and Noboru on the pier were trapped in the same viscous moment of time.

Finally, rocking the whole harbour and carrying to every city window; assailing kitchens with dinner on the stove, and shoddy hotel bedrooms where sheets are never changed, and desks waiting for children to come home, and schools and tennis courts and graveyards; plunging everything into a moment of grief and ruthlessly tearing even the hearts of the uninvolved, the *Rakuyo*'s siren screamed one last enormous farewell. Trailing white smoke, she sailed straight out to sea. Ryuji was lost from sight.

Part Two *Winter*

Chapter 1

At nine o'clock on the morning of the thirtieth of December, Ryuji emerged from the customs shed at Centre Pier. Fusako was there to meet him.

Centre Pier was a curious abstraction of a neighbourhood. The streets were unpeopled and excessively clean; the plane trees lining them were withered. Down a siding which ran between archaic red-brick warehouses and a pseudo-Renaissance shipping office chugged an ancient steam engine puffing clouds of black smoke. Even the little railway-crossing seemed unauthentic, as though it belonged to a set of toy trains. The sea was responsible for the unreality of the place, for it was to her service alone that the streets, the buildings, even the dumb bricks in the wall were pledged. The sea had simplified and abstracted to a point where the pier had lost its sense of reality and now seemed dazed, bereft of function.

Besides, it was raining. Rich cinnabar gushed out of the old brick walls and washed into puddles on the street. The masts spiring above the roofs were dripping wet.

Not wanting to attract attention, Fusako waited in the back seat of the car. Through the rain-streaked window she watched the crew emerge one by one from the weather-beaten wooden shed. Ryuji paused for a minute in the doorway to turn up the collar of his pea-jacket and pull his cap low over his eyes. Then he hunched into the rain, carrying an old zip-fastener bag. Fusako sent her chauffeur running out to call him.

He came hurtling into the car like a piece of bulky, rain-soaked baggage. 'I knew you'd come – I knew it,' he gasped, seizing the shoulders of Fusako's mink coat.

His cheeks were streaked with rain – or were those tears? – and he was more sunburned than before. Fusako had paled: her white face was like a window opened in the dim interior of the car. As they kissed, they were crying. Ryuji slipped his hands under Fusako's coat and clutched wildly at her body as though searching for life in a corpse he had saved from drowning, locked his arms around her supple waist and replenished his heart and mind with the details of her. It was only a six- or seven-minute ride to the house. Eventually, as the car was crossing Yamashita Bridge, they were able to begin a normal conversation.

'Thanks for all the letters. I read every one a hundred times.'

'I did yours too. You can stay with us at least over the New Year, can't you?'

'Thanks. . . . How's Noboru been?'

'He wanted to come and meet you at the pier but he caught a little cold and had to go to bed. Oh, it's nothing serious – hardly any temperature –'

The conversation was ordinary, remarks any landsmen might exchange, and it came easily. They had imagined during the months apart that their conversation would be difficult when they met again; restoring the bond between them to what it had been after three summer days had seemed impossible. Was it likely that things would proceed as smoothly as an arm slips into the sleeve of a coat unworn for half a year?

But the tears of joy had washed anxiety away and lifted them to a height where nothing was impossible. Ryuji was as if paralysed: the sight of familiar places, places they had visited together, failed to move him. That Yamashita Park and Marine Tower should now appear just as he had often pictured them seemed only obvious, inevitable. And the smoking drizzle of rain, by softening the too distinct scenery and making of it something closer to the images stored by memory, only heightened the reality of it all. Ryuji expected for some time after he disembarked to feel the world tottering precariously beneath his feet, and yet today more than ever before, like a piece in a jigsaw puzzle, he felt snugly in place in an anchored, amiable world.

They turned right off the bridge, drove for a short time along the canal, which was buried under grey tarpaulined barges, and began climbing the hill past the French Consulate. Far up in the sky, dishevelled clouds brightened and churned apart; the rain was letting up. They were at the top of the hill now, passing the entrance to the park. The car turned left into a lane and stopped in front of the Kuroda house. From the gate to the front door was only a few steps, but the tiled path was soaking wet. The old chauffeur held an umbrella over Fusako as he escorted her to the door and then rang the bell.

When the housekeeper appeared, Fusako told her to turn on the light in the vestibule. Ryuji stepped over the low sill and entered the dimness.

In the instant needed to cross the threshold, a subtle doubt assailed him. Presumably, the glittering ring they had re-entered together was just as they had left it. The difference was ineffably slight, but something, somewhere, had changed. Fusako had been careful never to allude to the future, neither when they had said good-bye at the end of the summer nor in any of her many letters, yet their embrace a few minutes before had made clear that it was here to this house, together, that both were longing to return. But Ryuji's eagerness wouldn't permit him to pause and consider the discrepancy further. He didn't even notice that he was entering an altogether different house.

'It's been simply pouring,' Fusako was saying. 'It seems to be letting up a little now, though.' Then the light in the vestibule clicked on and the imported marble floor floated into view.

A fire was blazing in the living-room fireplace, and installed on the mantelpiece in readiness for New Year's Day was a small wooden stand laden with oblatory rice-cakes and garlanded in the traditional manner with whitebeam and kelp and bunches of sea grapes. The housekeeper brought them some tea and managed a creditable greeting: 'It's very nice to see you back again. Noboru and Mrs Kuroda have been excited all the week.'

The only changes in the living-room were some new samples of Fusako's embroidery and a small tennis trophy on display in one corner. She guided Ryuji round the room, explaining each addition as she came to it. The moment he had sailed, her zeal for tennis and embroidery had increased. She had been playing at the club near the Myokoji Temple every weekend, sometimes even stealing away from the shop on weekday afternoons; the evenings she had spent alone in her room, embroidering on silk.

Many of her recent patterns had something to do with ships. The new cushions, completed during the autumn, were decorated with old-fashioned wheels and small stylized fleets of Portuguese schooners. The trophy was for women's doubles; she had won it in the club's end-of-the-year tournament. For Ryuji, all this was proof of her chastity during his absence.

'But nothing really exciting happened,' Fusako said. 'Not while you were away...'

She confessed how peeved she had been to discover herself waiting for him despite her determination not to. She had thrown herself into her work confident that he was forgotten, and when the last customer for the day had left and the shop was hushed, she would hear the fountain bubbling in the patio. And, listening, be struck with terror. Then she knew that she was waiting...

This time, Fusako was able to express herself with fluency and candour. The bold letters she had been writing week after week had granted her an unexpected new freedom. And Ryuji was more talkative than before, more animated. The change had started one day in Honolulu when he received Fusako's first letter. He became noticeably more friendly, even began to enjoy the natter sessions in the mess room. It wasn't long after that before the *Rakuyo*'s officers knew all the details of his love.

'Do you feel like going up and saying hello to Noboru? He was so excited about seeing you, I'll bet he didn't get a decent night's sleep either.'

Ryuji rose from his chair. It was clear now, beyond a doubt: he was the man they had been waiting for, the man they loved.

Taking a present for Noboru out of his suitcase, Ryuji followed Fusako up the same dark stairs he had climbed on trembling tiptoe that summer night. This time, his steps were the resolute tread of a man who belongs.

In bed upstairs, Noboru listened to the ascending footsteps. He was tense from waiting, his body under the covers stiff as a board, and yet, somehow, these weren't quite the footsteps he had expected.

There was a knock on his door and it swung open. Noboru saw a reddish-brown baby crocodile.

The beast hovered in the doorway, floating in the watery light which was pouring into the room from the sky outside, clear now and bright, and for an instant the glittering glass-bead eyes, and the gaping mouth, and the stiffened legs paddling the air, seemed to come alive. A question struggled through the confusion of his slightly feverish mind: has anyone ever used something living for a coat of arms? Once Ryuji had told him about the Coral Sea: the water inside an atoll was as still as the surface of a pond, but in the offing, huge waves thundered to pieces against the outer reef and the crashing crests of white foam looked like hugely distant phantoms. His headache, which, compared with yesterday's, had receded into the distance, was like a white crest billowing beyond the atoll. And the crocodile was the headache's coat of arms, the symbol of his own distant authority. It was true that sickness had touched the boy's face with majesty.

'Like him? He's for you.' Ryuji had been standing just outside the door, holding the crocodile at arm's length. Now he stepped into the room. He was wearing a grey turtleneck sweater; his face was deeply tanned.

Noboru had prepared for Ryuji's entrance by resolving not to smile with pleasure. Using illness as a pretext, he succeeded in maintaining a glum face.

'That's strange! He was so happy and excited just a

little while ago. Do you feel feverish again, dear?' An unwarranted little speech! Never before had his mother seemed such a petty person.

'There's a story attached to this,' Ryuji went on, unconscious of the tension in the room. He placed the beast next to Noboru's pillow. 'This crocodile was stuffed by the Indians in Brazil. Those tribesmen are real Indians. And when carnival time comes round, the warriors put crocodiles like this one or sometimes stuffed water fowl on their heads, in front of the feathers they wear in their hair. And they strap three little round mirrors to their foreheads. When those mirrors catch the light from the bonfires, they look just like . . . three-eyed devils. They string leopard teeth around their throats, and wrap themselves in leopard skins. And they all have quivers on their backs, and beautiful bows, and different-coloured arrows. Anyway, that's the story of this crocodile. It's part of the ceremonial dress the Brazilian Indians wear at carnival time.'

'Thanks,' Noboru said. He ran his hand over the glossy bumps on the crocodile's back and stroked the shrivelled limbs. Then he inspected the dust which had accumulated beneath the red glass-bead eyes while the beast had crouched on a shelf in some Brazilian country store, and thought about what Ryuji had said. The room was too hot; the sheets were feverish, wrinkled, damp. The bits of skin on the pillow had flaked off Noboru's dried lips. He had been picking at them furtively a few minutes before. Just as he began to worry that his lips might look too red, he glanced involuntarily towards the drawer that concealed the peephole. Now he had done it! He was in agony. What if the adults traced his gaze and levelled suspicious eyes on the wall? But no, it was all right. They were even more insensible than he had suspected: they were cradled in the numbing arms of love.

Noboru stared hard at the sailor. His sun-blackened face looked even more virile than before, the thick eyebrows and white teeth more sharply accented. But Noboru had sensed something unnatural about the sailor's monologue, a forced attempt to relate to his own fancies, a truckling to the exaggerated sentiments he had set down in his frequent letters. There was something counterfeit about this Ryuji. When he couldn't bear it any longer, Noboru spoke. 'I don't know – there's something phony about this . . .'

'Are you kidding? Because he's so small?' It was a good-natured misunderstanding. 'Even crocodiles are small when they're kids. Try going to the zoo some time.'

'Noboru! I'm surprised at you. Now why don't you stop being so impolite and show Mr Tsukazaki your stamp album.'

But before he could move a hand, his mother had snatched the album from the desk and was showing Ryuji the carefully mounted stamps he had mailed to Noboru from ports around the world.

She sat in the chair with her face towards the light and turned the pages while Ryuji, one arm across the chair, looked over her shoulder. Noboru noticed they both had handsome profiles: the thin, clear winter light silvered the bridges of their noses. They seemed oblivious of his presence in the room.

'Mr Tsukazaki, when will you be sailing again?' Noboru asked abruptly.

His mother turned to him with a shocked face and he could see that she had paled. It was the question she most wanted to ask, and most dreaded. Ryuji was posing near the window with his back to them. He half-closed his eyes, and then, very slowly, said: 'I'm not sure yet.'

Noboru was stunned. Fusako didn't speak, but she looked like a bottle full of feeling which boiled against the small cork stopper. Her expression might have meant joy or sorrow – a woman's sodden face. To Noboru, she looked like a washerwoman.

A brief pause, and Ryuji again spoke calmly. His tone was sympathetic, the compassion a man feels when he is certain he holds the power to affect another's fate: 'At any rate, it'll take at least until after the New Year to get the ship unloaded . . .'

Red with rage and coughing violently, Noboru pulled his diary from under the pillow as soon as they had left, and wrote a short entry.

CHARGES AGAINST RYUJI TSUKAZAKI

THREE: *answering, when I asked when he would be sailing again: 'I'm not sure yet.'*

Noboru put down his pen and thought for a minute while his anger mounted. Then he added:

FOUR: *coming back here again in the first place.*

But soon he began to feel ashamed of his anger. What good had been all that training in 'absolute dispassion'? He carefully explored every corner of his heart to make certain not even a fragment of rage remained, and then re-read what he had written. When he had finished, he was convinced: revision would not be necessary.

Then he heard a stirring in the next room. Apparently his mother had gone into the bedroom. Ryuji seemed to be there too . . . the door to his own room wasn't locked.

Part Two

Noboru's heart began to hammer. How, he wondered, in an unlocked room at this time of morning could he quickly – that was important – remove the drawer and steal into the space in the wall without being discovered?

Chapter 2

Fusako's present was an armadillo pocketbook. It was a bizarre affair, with a handle that looked like a rat's neck, and crude clasps and stitching, but she left the house with it happily and displayed it proudly at the shop while Mr Shibuya scowled his disapproval.

They spent the last day of the year apart: Fusako was needed at Rex and Ryuji had to take the afternoon watch. This time it seemed perfectly natural that they should go separate ways for half a day.

It was after ten when Fusako returned that evening. Ryuji had been helping Noboru and the housekeeper with the traditional New Year's Eve cleaning and together they had managed to finish the job more quickly than in previous years. Ryuji issued brisk instructions as though he were directing a scrub-down on the deck, and Noboru, whose temperature had come down that morning, carried out his orders with enthusiasm.

Fusako came in as they were descending the stairs with mops and pails after having cleaned all the upstairs rooms. Ryuji had rolled up the sleeves of his sweater and bound a towel around his head; Noboru was turbaned in the same fashion, his cheeks flushed and glowing. The scene surprised and delighted Fusako, but she couldn't help worrying a little about Noboru's health.

'Stop worrying so much! Working up a good sweat's the best way to kill a cold.' The remark may have been crude as an attempt at reassurance but at least it was 'man's talk', something Fusako's house hadn't heard for a long time. The walls and the old beams in the ceiling seemed to shrink from the masculine utterance.

When the whole family had gathered to listen to the midnight bells and feast on special buckwheat noodles, the housekeeper told an anecdote from her past which she repeated every New Year's Eve: 'At the Macgregors' – that's the people I used to work for – New Year's Eve always meant a big party with lots of company. And at twelve o'clock on the dot everybody started kissing everybody else like nothing on earth! One time I even had an old Irish gentleman with whiskers smooch me on the cheek – he just hung on there like he was a leech or something...'

Ryuji embraced Fusako as soon as they were alone in the bedroom. Later, when the first pale promise of dawn appeared, he proposed something childish: why didn't they walk over to the park and watch the first sunrise of the New Year? Fusako was captivated by the lunacy of racing into the cold. She jumped out of bed and bundled herself into everything she could get on – tights, slacks, a cashmere sweater, and a gorgeous Danish ski sweater over that; and tiptoeing down the stairs, they unlocked the front door and stepped outside.

The dawn air felt good against their heated bodies. Racing into the deserted park, they laughed out loud and chased each other in and out among the fir trees, and took deep breaths, vying to see who could exhale the whitest steam into the cold, dark air. They felt as though thin crusts of ice were coating their love-staled mouths.

Part Two

It was well past six when they leaned against the railing that overlooked the harbour: Venus had banked into the south. Though the lights of buildings and the red lamps blinking on distant masts were still bright, and though the beacon's red and green blades of light still knifed through the darkness in the park, outlines of houses could be discerned and the sky was touched with reddish purple.

Small and distant, the first cock call of the year reached them on the chill morning wind, a tragic, fitful cry. 'May this be a good year for us all.' Fusako spoke her prayer aloud. It was cold, and when she nestled her cheek against Ryuji's he kissed the lips so close to his and said: 'It will be. It has to be.'

Gradually a blurred form at the water's edge was sharpening into a building. As Ryuji stared at a red bulb blooming above an emergency exit, he became painfully conscious of the texture of shore life. He would be thirty-four in May. It was time to abandon the dream he had cherished too long. Time to realize that no specially tailored glory was waiting for him, no matter if the feeble eaves lamps still defied the green-grey light of morning by refusing to come awake, to open his eyes.

Though it was New Year's Day, a submerged tremolo pervaded the harbour. Every few minutes a barge unravelled from the moored fleet and hacked dryly down the canal. As a rosy hue stained the surface of the water and seemed to inflate itself into a round abundance, the poles of light slanting away from anchored ships began to dwindle. Twenty minutes past six: the mercury lamps in the park clicked out.

'Are you getting cold?' Ryuji asked.

'My gums are stinging, it's so cold – but I don't mind. The sun will be coming up any minute now.'

Are you getting cold? . . . Are you getting cold? Ryuji asked again and again, and all the time he was directing another question to himself: Are you really going to give it up? *The feeling of the sea, the dark, drunken feeling that unearthly rolling always brings? The thrill of saying good-bye? The sweet tears you weep for your song? Are you going to give up the life which has detached you from the world, kept you remote, impelled you towards the pinnacle of manliness?* The secret yearning for death. The glory beyond and the death beyond. Everything was 'beyond', wrong or right, had always been 'beyond'. *Are you going to give that up?* His heart in spasm because he was always in contact with the ocean's dark swell and the lofty light from the edge of the clouds, twisting, withering until it clogged and then swelling up again, and he unable to distinguish the most exalted feelings from the meanest and that not mattering really since he could hold the sea responsible – *are you going to give up that luminous freedom?*

And yet Ryuji had discovered on the return leg of his last voyage that he was tired, tired to death of the squalor and the boredom in a sailor's life. He was convinced that he had tasted it all, even the lees, and he was glutted. What a fool he'd been! There was no glory to be found, not anywhere in the world. Not in the Northern Hemisphere. Not in the Southern Hemisphere. Not even beneath that constellation every sailor dreams about, the Southern Cross!

Now they could make out the lumber yards beyond the canal; roosters had crowed at the sky until a coy blush spread across her face. Finally the mast lamps blinked out and ships withdrew like phantoms into the fog that shrouded the harbour. Then, as an angry red began to smoulder along the edges of the sky, the open park behind them unfurled into whitish emptiness and the skirts on the beacon beam fell away, leaving only glinting needlepoints of red and green light.

It was very cold; leaning against the railing with their arms round each other, they stamped their feet.

'It can't be long now,' Fusako said, her voice rising above the chatter of small birds. The lipstick she had dabbed on before they left the house, a spot of vivid red rising out of the whiteness of her chilled, drawn face, looked beautiful to Ryuji.

A minute later, far to the right of the floating lumber and surprisingly high up, a gauzy red ring loomed in the slate-grey sky. Immediately the sun became a globe of pure red but still so weak they could look straight at it, a blood-red moon.

'I know this will be a good year; it couldn't be anything else with us here like this, watching the first sunrise together. And you know something? This is the first time I've ever seen the sunrise on New Year's Day.' Fusako's voice shrivelled in the cold. Ryuji heard himself bellow in the resolute voice he used to shout orders into the wind on the winter deck: 'Will you marry me?'

'What?'

Annoyed at having to repeat himself, he blurted out things better left unsaid: 'I'm asking you to marry me. I may be just a dumb sailor but I've never done anything I'm ashamed of. You may laugh when I say this, but I have nearly two million yen saved up – you can see my bankbook presently. That's everything I have to my name and I'm going to give it all to you whether you marry me or not.'

His artless proposal touched the worldly woman more deeply than he knew. Overjoyed, Fusako began to cry.

The sun was blazing now, too dazzlingly bright for Ryuji's anxious eyes, and the whistle-wailing, gear-grinding cacophony of the harbour was surging towards full pitch. The horizon was misted over, the sun's reflection spreading like a reddish haze over the surface of the water.

'Yes – of course I will. But I think there are some problems we ought to discuss first. There's Noboru, for example, and my work at the shop. Can I make just one condition? What you've just said, I mean – if you're planning to leave again soon – it would be hard . . .'

'I won't be sailing again for a while. As a matter of fact . . .' Ryuji faltered, and was silent.

There wasn't a single Japanese room in Fusako's house; her mode of living was thoroughly Western except on New Year's Day, when she observed tradition by serving the special New Year's breakfast on lacquered trays and drinking toasts with spiced *sake*.

Ryuji hadn't slept at all. He washed his face with 'young water', the first water drawn in the year, and went into the dining-room. It was a strange feeling, as though he were still in Europe, at the Japanese Consulate in some northern seaport. In the past, he and the other officers of the *Rakuyo* had been invited to New Year's breakfast at consulates abroad; the *sake* dipper and the wooden cups stacked on a stand inlaid with gold, and the lacquered boxes filled with traditional side dishes, were always arrayed on a table in a bright Western dining-room just as they were here.

Part Two

Noboru came down wearing a new tie, and New Year's congratulations were exchanged. In previous years Noboru had always drunk the first toast, but when the time came and he reached for the uppermost and smallest of the three cups, Fusako stopped him with a reproving look.

Pretending to be embarrassed, he simpered:

'It seems pretty silly for Mr Tsukazaki to drink out of the smallest.' But his eyes never left the cup. It seemed to wither in the grasp of the huge, calloused hand that carried it to the sailor's lips. Buried under the thick fingers of a hand accustomed to grappling rope, the vermilion plum-branch cup looked horribly vulgar.

When he had finished the toast, Ryuji began an account of a hurricane in the Caribbean before Noboru even had a chance to coax him:

'When the pitching gets really bad you can hardly cook your rice. But you manage somehow and then eat it plain, just squeezed into little balls. Of course, the bowls won't stay put on a table, so you push the desks in the saloon up against the wall and sit on the floor and try to gulp it down.

'But this hurricane in the Caribbean was really something. The *Rakuyo* was built overseas more than twenty years ago and she starts leaking when you hit rough weather. Well, this time the water came pouring in around the rivet holes in the hull. And at a time like that there's no difference between officers and deck-hands, everybody works together like drowning rats, bailing and throwing mats down and pouring cement as fast as you can get it mixed. And even if you get slammed against a wall or hurled into the dark when the power cuts out, you haven't got time to be scared.

'I'll tell you one thing, though: no matter how long you've been on a ship, you never get used to storms. I mean you're sure every time you run into one that your number is up. Anyway, the day before this last hurricane the sunset looked too much like a big fire and the red in the sky was kind of murky and the water was quiet as a lake. I had a sort of feeling then that something was coming –'

'Stop it, please stop!' Fusako screamed, clapping her hands over her ears. 'Please don't talk about things like that any more.'

His mother's histrionics annoyed Noboru: why did she have to cover her ears and protest about an adventure story which was obviously being told for his benefit? Or had it been intended mainly for her?

The thought made him uncomfortable. Ryuji had told the same sort of sea story before, but this time his delivery seemed different. The tone of his voice reminded Noboru of a pedlar selling sundry wares while he handled them with dirty hands. Unsling a pack from your back and spread it open on the ground for all to see: one hurricane Caribbean-style – scenery along the banks of the Panama Canal – a carnival smeared in red dust from the Brazilian countryside – a tropical rainstorm flooding a village in the twinkling of an eye – bright parrots hollering beneath a dark sky. . . . No doubt about it: Ryuji did have a pack of wares.

Chapter 3

On the fifth of January the *Rakuyo* sailed and Ryuji was not aboard. He stayed on as a guest in the Kuroda house.

Rex opened on the sixth. Relieved and in high spirits because Ryuji had stayed behind, Fusako arrived at the shop just before noon and received New Year's congratulations from Mr Shibuya and the rest of the staff. Waiting on her desk was an invoice from an English distributor:

Messrs Rex Ltd, Yokohama
ORDER NO. 1062–B

The shipment had arrived during the vacation on the *El Dorado*; there were two and a half dozen men's vests and pullovers, and a dozen and a half pairs of sports trousers, sizes 34, 38, and 40. Including the ten per cent commission for the distributor, the bill came to ninety thousand yen. Even if they shelved the order for a month or so they could count on clearing fifty thousand yen in profits: half the merchandise was on special order and could be sold at any time. And not having to worry about depreciation no matter how long the rest remained on the shelf was the advantage of handling English products through a first-rate distributor. The retail prices were established in England and their account would be cancelled if they tried to undersell.

Mr Shibuya came into the office and announced: 'The Jackson Company is having a pre-season showing of their spring and summer collections on the twenty-fifth. We have received an invitation.'

'Oh? I suppose that means we'll be competing with buyers from the big Tokyo stores again – not that those people aren't all blind as bats.'

'They have no feel for fabric or design because they have never worn fine clothes themselves.'

'True enough!' Fusako noted the date in the memo book on her desk. 'Is it tomorrow that we're supposed to go to the Foreign Trade Ministry? Bureaucrats always make me so nervous, I'll probably just sit there and grin. I'm counting on you to get us through.'

'I'll do what I can. One of the senior clerks happens to be an old friend.'

'Oh yes, you've mentioned that before – I feel better already.'

Hoping to satisfy the tastes of some new customers, Rex had entered into a special agreement with the Men's Town and Country Shop in New York: letters of credit had already been issued and now it was up to Fusako to apply through the Ministry of External Trade for an import licence.

'I've been meaning to ask,' Fusako said abruptly, her eyes on the V neck of the thin old dandy's camel-hair vest, 'how you've been feeling lately.'

'Not too well, thank you. I imagine it's my arthritis playing up again, but the pain seems to be spreading.'

'Well, have you been to see a doctor?'

'No, what with the holiday rush and everything . . .'

'But you haven't been feeling well since before the New Year.'

'I don't have time to waste sitting around in a doctor's office, especially this time of year.'

'I still wish you'd get someone to look at you right

away. If anything happened to you, we'd be out of business.'

The old man smiled vaguely, one wrinkled white hand fussing nervously with the tight knot in his tie.

A salesgirl came in to say that Miss Yoriko Kasuga had arrived.

Fusako went down to the patio. This time Yoriko had come alone. She was wearing a mink coat and peering into a showcase with her back turned. When she had decided on some Lancôme lipstick and a Pelican fountain pen, Fusako invited her to lunch; the famous actress beamed with pleasure. Fusako took her to Le Centaure, a small French restaurant near the harbour where yachtsmen often gathered. The proprietor was an old gourmet who had once worked at the French Consulate.

Fusako looked at the actress as though to measure the loneliness of this simple, stolid woman. Yoriko had received not one of the awards she had been counting on for the past year, and obviously her excursion to Yokohama today was an escape from the eyes society levels on a star who has failed to win an award. Though she must have had followers beyond counting, the only person with whom she could be frank and at ease was the proprietress of a Yokohama luxury shop, not even a close friend.

Fusako decided it would be best not to mention film awards during lunch.

They drank a bottle of the restaurant's celebrated *vin de maison* with their *bouillabaisse*. Fusako had to order for Yoriko because she couldn't read the French menu.

'You know, Mama, you're really beautiful,' the heavily-built beauty said abruptly. 'I'd give anything to look like you.' Yoriko slighted her own beauty more than any woman Fusako knew. The actress had marvellous breasts, gorgeous eyes, a fine-sculptured nose, and voluptuous lips, yet she was tormented by vague feelings of inferiority. She even believed, and it pained her not a little, that the awards committee had passed her by because men watching her on the screen saw only a woman they would love to take to bed.

Fusako watched the famous, beautiful, unhappy woman flush with contentment as she decorated her name in an autograph book produced by the waitress. Yoriko's reaction to an autograph book was always a good indication of her mood. And judging from the drunken generosity with which she was flourishing her pen just now, a fan would need only to ask for one of her breasts to receive it.

'The only people in this world I really trust are my fans – even if they do forget you so quickly,' Yoriko mumbled as she lit a woman's cigarette.

'Don't you trust me?' Fusako teased. She could predict Yoriko's felicitous response to such a question.

'Do you think I'd come all the way to Yokohama if I didn't? You're the only real friend I have. Honestly, you are. I haven't felt so relaxed for ages and it's all thanks to you, Mama.' That name again! Fusako winced.

The walls of the restaurant were decorated with watercolour paintings of famous yachts, bright red chequered tablecloths covered the empty tables; they were the only people in the small room. The old window frames began to creak in the wind and a page of a newspaper scudded down the empty street. The window opened on a dismal stretch of ashen warehouse walls.

Yoriko kept her mink coat draped round her shoulders while she ate; an imposing necklace of heavy gold chain swayed on her stately chest. She had escaped the

scandal-loving world, she had even eluded her own ambi-
tion, and now, like a muscular woman labourer lazing in
the sun between wearisome tasks, she was content. Though
her reasons for sorrow or joy rarely seemed convincing to
the observer, it was at moments like this that the source of
her vitality became apparent. She derived her strength
from something she herself was least aware of: her beauty.

Fusako had a sudden feeling that she would find in
Yoriko the ideal confidante. So she began to tell her about
Ryuji, and the happiness in the story made her so drunk
that she revealed every intimate detail.

'Is that right! And did he really give you his seal and
a bankbook with two million yen on deposit?'

'I tried to refuse, but he wouldn't take no for an answer.'

'But there was no reason for you to refuse. And wasn't
that a manly thing to do! Of course, the money is chicken-
feed as far as you're concerned, but it's the spirit behind
it that counts. I would never have dreamed that there
were men like that around any more. Especially since the
only men who come near me are scroungers out for whatever they can get. I hope you realize how lucky you are.'

Fusako had never dreamed that Yoriko could be prac-
tical and she was astonished when, having listened to the
whole story, the actress promptly prescribed a course of
action.

A prerequisite of any marriage, she began, was an investigation by a private detective agency. Fusako would
need a photograph of Ryuji and about thirty thousand
yen. If she hurried the agency she could have the results
within a week. Yoriko would be happy to recommend a
reliable one.

Though she didn't imagine there was any cause for
worry in this case, there was always the possibility that

a sailor might have an ugly disease: it would be best if they exchanged health certificates, Ryuji accompanying Fusako to a doctor of her choice.

Inasmuch as the new relationship was between father and son and would not involve the question of a step-mother, there would be no serious problems where Noboru was concerned. And since Ryuji was hero-worshipped by the boy (and seemed to be basically a gentleman), they were certain to get on.

It would be a bad mistake to allow Ryuji to remain idle any longer. If Fusako intended to train Ryuji to take over Rex some day, she would be wise to start him learning the business and helping around the shop at once, particularly since Shibuya, the manager, was beginning to show his age.

Finally, though his gesture with the bankbook had made clear that there was nothing mercenary about Ryuji, the fact remained that the shipping slump had brought maritime stocks crashing, and it was obvious besides that he had been looking for a way out of his career as a seaman; Fusako would have to be careful not to compromise herself just because she was a widow. It was up to her to insist on an equal relationship, to make certain she was not being used.

Yoriko pressed each point home firmly but with patience, as if she were trying to persuade a child, though in fact Fusako was the older. Fusako was amazed to hear a woman she had considered a fool talk such good sense.

'I never realized you were so' – there was new respect in her voice – 'so capable.'

'It's easy once you find out what they're up to. A year or so ago there was a man I thought I wanted to marry. And I told one of our producers the whole story. Maybe you've heard of him. Tatsuo Muragoshi? He's one of the best in the business. Anyway, it was just like him not to mention my work or my rating or even my contract. He just smiled the warmest smile you've ever seen and congratulated me and then he advised me to do all the things I've just told you to do. It seemed like such a nuisance, I left everything to him. Well, in one week I found out that a certain person was seeing three women and had already fathered two bastards, and that wasn't all: he was sick, if you know what I mean. He had never held a decent job for long, and it looked as if he was planning to kick the rest of my family out as soon as we got married so he could sit around swilling beer while I supported us both. What do you think of that? That's men for you. Not that there aren't exceptions . . .'

From that moment Fusako loathed the actress, and her hatred was charged with the indignation of an honest, respectable bourgeois. She took Yoriko's unwitting innuendo not only as an attack on Ryuji but also as an insult to her own family and upbringing, and an affront to the refined traditions of the Kuroda house which amounted to a slur on her dead husband's honour.

In the first place, their backgrounds were entirely different, and there was no reason why her love affair should develop in a pattern familiar to Yoriko. *Sooner or later I'm going to have to make her understand. There's nothing I can do now, though, because she's just a customer, not a friend.*

Fusako didn't notice that the position she was taking in her rage was a contradiction of that violent summer passion. Deep inside, she was angry not so much for her dead husband as for the respectable household she had maintained for herself and her son since his death. And

Yoriko's insinuation had sounded like the thing she dreaded most, society's first thrust of reproach at her 'indiscretion'. Now, just as an appropriate 'happy ending' was about to atone for that indiscretion, Yoriko had cast a pall over it. Purposely! Angry for her dead husband, angry for the Kuroda house, angry for Noboru – goaded by every anger that apprehension can breed, Fusako paled.

If Ryuji were really an opportunist with all kinds of dreadful secrets, I would never have fallen in love with him. Yoriko may be a gullible fool, but I happen to have a sound sense of what's good and what's bad. The thought was equivalent to a denial of that unaccountable summer passion, yet the whispering inside her began suddenly to seethe, to swell until it threatened to burst out.

Unaware of her friend's agitation, Yoriko sipped her coffee contentedly. Abruptly, as though she had remembered something, she set the cup in its saucer and, turning back the cuff of her left sleeve, pointed to the white inner side of her wrist.

'You must promise to keep this a secret. I wouldn't tell anyone but you, Mama. It's the scar from that time I was supposed to get married – I tried to kill myself with a razor blade.'

'That's strange – I don't remember seeing anything about it in the papers,' Fusako taunted, herself again.

'No, because Mr Muragoshi ran all over the city and managed to keep the news hushed up. But it bled and bled.'

Yoriko held her arm up in front of her and touched the wrist pityingly with her lips before entrusting it to Fusako for inspection. You had to look closely to see them at all, a few irregular whitish scars that must have been shallow, tentative cuts. Fusako felt only contempt. And she made a point of searching Yoriko's wrist as though unable to locate the scars at all. Then she knit sympathetic brows and said, becoming the proprietress of Rex again: 'What a dreadful thing! Can you imagine how many people all over Japan would have wept if you'd succeeded. A lovely girl like you – such a waste. Promise me you'll never do anything like that again.'

'Of course I won't, Mama, a stupid thing like that. Those people you said would cry for me are all I have to live for. Would you cry for me, Mama?'

'Crying wouldn't begin to be enough,' Fusako crooned, 'but let's talk about something more pleasant.'

Ordinarily, Fusako would have considered going to a private detective agency an inauspicious beginning, but now she was determined out of spite to receive a favourable report from the same people who had damned Yoriko's prospective husband.

'You know what?' she began. 'I have to go up to Tokyo with Mr Shibuya tomorrow anyway, and when we've finished what we have to do I think I'll get rid of him and drop in at that investigation service you mentioned. If you could just write me a note of introduction?'

'Delighted.' Yoriko took out the fountain pen she had just bought and, fumbling through the contents of her alligator pocketbook, came up with a small white card.

A week and a day later Fusako had a long telephone conversation with Yoriko. She sounded proud: 'I just wanted to call and thank you, I'm so grateful. I did just as you suggested . . . yes, a great success. The report is really very interesting. Thirty thousand yen is cheap when you consider all the trouble they must have taken.

Would you like to hear it? I mean, do you have a minute? Do me a favour then and let me read it to you:

'"Special Investigation – Confidential Report. The following are the findings of an investigation into the affairs of Ryuji Tsukazaki as stipulated by the client.

'"One: particulars as indicated – subject's criminal record, relations with women, etc. Particulars of the subject's personal history coincide precisely with information in the client's possession. The mother, Masako, died when the subject was ten years of age. The father, Hajime, was employed as a clerk in the Katsushita Ward Office in Tokyo. He did not remarry after his wife's death, devoting himself to raising and educating his only son. The family home was destroyed in an air raid in March of 1945. The subject's sister, Yoshiko, died of typhus in May of the same year. The subject graduated from the merchant-marine high school . . ."

'It goes on and on that way. Isn't the writing terrible? Let me skip ahead: ". . . as for the subject's relations with women, he is not at present involved with a woman nor is there any indication that he has ever cohabited with a woman or even engaged in a prolonged or significant affair . . ."

'That's really summing it up, wouldn't you say!

'". . . though the subject displays slightly eccentric tendencies, he is conscientious about his work, highly responsible, and extremely healthy: he has never had a serious illness. Results of the investigation to date show no history of mental illness or other hereditary disease in the immediate family . . .'

'There was one more thing – yes, here it is: "The subject has no debts; he has never borrowed in advance of his salary nor has he ever owed money to his employer.

Part Two

All indications point to a spotless financial record. The subject is known to prefer solitude to company and has never been at ease socially; accordingly, he does not always get on well with his colleagues . . ."

'As long as we get on well that's all that matters. Oh? Someone at the door? I'll let you go then. I just wanted to thank you for being so very kind, I'm truly grateful. I hope we'll be seeing you at the shop again soon . . . Ryuji? Yes, he's been coming in every day since last week, just as you suggested. You know, getting to know his way around. You'll meet him next time you come down . . . yes . . . yes, I will. And thanks again. Good-bye.'

Chapter 4

School began on the eleventh but classes were over at noon. The gang hadn't met at all during the vacation. The Chief hadn't even been in town: his parents had dragged him off on a sightseeing trip to Kyoto and Nara. Together again at last, they decided after eating lunch at school that the tip of Yamashita Pier, which was always deserted, would be a good place for a meeting.

'You fellows probably think it's freezing out there. Everybody does, but they're all wrong,' the Chief announced. 'There happens to be a very good windbreak. You'll see when we get there.'

Since noon the sky had been cloudy and it was getting colder. The north wind, blowing down on them as they walked out along the pier, burned like icy fire.

Reclamation of the foreshore had been completed but one of the new docks was still under construction. The sea was undulating greyly; three buoys, washed by endless waves, were bobbing up and down. The only distinct objects in the murky factory jungle across the harbour were the five chimneys of an electric power plant; brackish yellow smoke struggled above the blurred line of factory rooftops. Beyond and far to the left of the dock, the pair of squat red-and-white lighthouses which formed the gateway to the harbour looked from here like a single column.

Moored at the dock in front of the shed to the right of them was a five- or six-thousand-ton freighter in terrible disrepair, a grey banner drooping from the stern. On the far side of the shed, in a berth they couldn't see, a foreign ship was apparently at anchor. The swaying of her beautiful white spars, which spired above the shed, was the only bright motion in the gloomy scene.

They saw immediately what the Chief's windbreak was. Piled from the warehouse to the edge of the sea-wall was a jumbled village of green-and-silver packing crates, each large enough to accommodate a small cow. Large plywood boxes reinforced with tough steel bands and stamped with the names of foreign exporters, they had been left on the pier to rot.

The boys whooped down on the village and began a wild free-for-all, lurking between crates and leaping out in flying tackles or chasing each other in and out among the disordered rows. They were all soaked with sweat by the time the Chief discovered at the very centre of the village a large crate that was to his liking: two of the sides had fallen away but the steel band was still intact and the contents had been removed down to the last wisp of wood shavings.

Shouting in a shrike's voice, the Chief assembled the

scattered band inside the crate. Three sat on the floor, three stood in the corners, arms resting on the steel band. They felt as if their outlandish vehicle was about to ascend on the arm of a crane into the cloudy winter sky.

Scribblings covered the plywood walls; they read each of them aloud: LET'S MEET IN YAMASHITA PARK — FORGET IT ALL AND TRY HAVING SOME FUN . . . like linked verses in a classical poem, each line was a clever distortion of the hopes and dreams in the preceding line: WE NEED TO FALL IN LOVE, PAL — FORGET WOMEN. WHO NEEDS THEM? — DON'T NEVER FORGET YOUR DREAM — GOT A BLACK SCAR ON MY BLUE BLUE HEART. . . peeping out of a corner was a young sailor's trembling soul: I HAVE CHANGED. I'M A NEW MAN. A freighter sketched in black let fly four arrow markers: the arrow at the left indicated YOKOHAMA, the arrow at the right, NEW YORK; the third arrow aspired to HEAVEN and the last plummeted towards HELL. Scrawled in English capitals and emphatically circled were the words ALL FORGET, and there was a self-portrait, a sailor with mournful eyes wearing a pea-jacket with upturned collar and smoking a seaman's pipe. The story was of the sailor's loneliness and his longings, and it was told with self-importance and overwhelming melancholy. Too stereotyped to be true. A sadly determined exaggeration of his qualifications for dreaming about himself.

'This crap's all lies,' the Chief said angrily. Doubling his powerless white hand into a fist he pummelled the plywood wall. His small hand was for all of the boys a symbol of despair. Now they were rejected even by lies. But hadn't the Chief said once that there was a label called 'impossibility' pasted all over the world, that they were the only ones who could tear it off once and for all?

'What's your hero been up to since last time? Well, Number Three? There's a rumour going around that he's come back . . .' The Chief felt every eye on him and his voice was cold, venomous. As he spoke, he pulled out of the pockets of his overcoat a pair of leather gloves and, smoothing them over his fingers, turned back the cuffs just enough for the fluffy bright-red lining to show.

'He's back,' Noboru admitted, wishing the subject hadn't come up.

'And? Did he do anything *terrific* during this last trip?'

'Well . . . yes! He ran into a hurricane in the Caribbean.'

'Is that right! I suppose he got soaked like a drowned rat? Like that time he took a shower in the drinking fountain at the park?'

At this everyone laughed and laughed. Noboru knew he was being ridiculed, but he quickly regained his pride and was able to report on Ryuji's activities as though he were describing the habits of an insect.

The sailor had lolled around the house until the seventh. When Noboru learned that the *Rakuyo* had sailed on the fifth, he was stunned. This man, so at one with the *Rakuyo*'s existence, so inseparably a part of the receding lustre of a ship, had sundered himself from that beautiful whole, wilfully banished from his dream the phantoms of ships and the sea!

Naturally Noboru stuck close to Ryuji during the holiday and listened to sea stories by the hour, gaining a knowledge of sailing none of the others could match. What he wanted, though, was not that knowledge but the green drop the sailor would leave behind when some day, in the very middle of a story, he started up in agitation and soared out to sea again.

Part Two

The phantoms of the sea and ships and ocean voyages existed only in that glistening green drop. But with each new day, another of the abominable odours of shore routine adhered to the sailor: the odour of home, the odour of neighbours, the odour of peace, odours of fish frying and pleasantries and furniture that never budged, the odour of household budget books and weekend excursions . . . all the putrid odours landsmen reek of, the stench of death.

Then began the laborious projects: Ryuji read the silly novels and art books recommended by Fusako, and studied English conversation, a class each night on television and a text empty of nautical terms; he listened to Fusako's lectures on problems of store management; he learned to wear the 'smart' English clothes she lavished on him; he had suits tailored, and vests, and overcoats; and then, from the eighth of January, he began going to the shop every day. That first morning, natty in a new suit of English tweed they had rushed to have ready in time, cheerful, expectant, eager . . .

'Eager.' Noboru spoke the word as though he had ice on the tip of his tongue.

'Eager,' mimicked Number Two.

The boys stopped laughing as they listened. Gradually they realized how grave the situation was. It seemed to indicate the end of a dream they shared, and its replacement by a bleak, dreary future. And maybe they had been wrong: maybe there was no such thing as the ultimate after all.

Through a narrow gap between two crates, they glimpsed a motor launch knifing whitecaps as it angled across the harbour. The whine of the engine hovered over the water long after the boat was out of sight.

'Number Three,' the Chief began, leaning languidly against the plywood wall, 'would you like to make that sailor a hero again?'

Suddenly Noboru felt cold; he crouched and began to toy with the pointed tips of his shoes. The answer when it finally came was an evasion: 'But you know, he still keeps his sailor cap and his pea-jacket and even his dirty old turtleneck sweater folded away in his cupboard. You can tell he doesn't want to throw them away.'

'There's just one way to make him a hero again,' the Chief continued, giving no indication that he had heard Noboru, 'but I can't tell you what it is yet. The time will come, though, and soon.'

The others were forbidden to probe for the answer when the Chief chose to speak in riddles. Effortlessly changing the subject, he focused the conversation on himself.

'Let me tell you about my holiday. On this trip we took, I was rubbing noses with my people every day from morning to night for the first time in quite a while. Fathers! Just think about it for a minute – they're enough to make you puke. Fathers are evil itself, laden with everything ugly in Man.

'There is no such thing as a good father because the role itself is bad. Strict fathers, soft fathers, nice moderate fathers – one's as bad as another. They stand in the way of our progress while they try to burden us with their inferiority complexes, and their unrealizéd aspirations, and their resentments, and their ideals, and the weaknesses they've never told anyone about, and their sins, and their sweeter-than-honey dreams, and the maxims they've never had the courage to live by – they'd like to unload all that silly crap on us, all of it! Even the most neglectful fathers, like mine, are no different. Their consciences hurt them because they've never paid any attention to their children and they want the kids to understand just how bad the pain is – to sympathize!

'On New Year's Day we went to Arashi Yama in Kyoto and as we were crossing the Bridge of Moons I asked my old man a question: "Dad, is there any purpose in life?" You see what I was getting at, don't you, what I really meant? *Father, can you give me one single reason why you go on living? Wouldn't it be better just to fade away as quickly as possible?* But a first-class insinuation never reaches a man like that. He just looked surprised and his eyes popped and he stared at me. I hate that kind of ridiculous adult surprise. And when he finally answered, what do you think he said? "Son, nobody is going to provide you with a purpose in life; you've got to make one for yourself."

'How's that for a stupid, hackneyed moral! He just pressed a button and out came one of the things fathers are supposed to say. And did you ever look at a father's eyes at a time like that? They're suspicious of anything creative, anxious to whittle the world down into something puny they can handle. A father is a reality-concealing machine, a machine for dishing up lies to kids, and that isn't even the worst of it: secretly he believes that he represents reality.

'Fathers are the flies of this world. They hover round our heads waiting for a chance, and when they see something rotten, they buzz in and root in it. Filthy, lecherous flies broadcasting to the whole world that they've screwed our mothers. And there's nothing they won't do to contaminate our freedom and our ability. Nothing they won't do to protect the filthy cities they've built for themselves.'

'My old man still won't buy me an air rifle,' Number Two murmured, his arms round his knees.

'And he never will, either. But it's time you realized that a father who would buy you an air rifle is just as bad as one who won't.'

'My father beat me again yesterday. That makes the third time since the New Year.'

'Beat you?' Noboru repeated in horror.

'He slaps me across the face. Sometimes he even punches.'

'Why don't you do something?'

''Cause I'm not strong enough to take him on.'

'Then you should – why don't you' – Noboru's face was bright red and he was shouting – 'butter his toast with potassium cyanide or something like that!'

'There are worse things than being beaten.' The Chief's thin red upper lip curled. 'There are lots of things worse than that, only you don't know about them. You're one of the fortunate ones. When your father died your case became special. But you've got to know about the evil in the world too; otherwise you'll never have any real power.'

'My old man is always coming home drunk and bullying my mother,' Number Four said. 'And when I stood up for her one time he got white as a sheet and grinned and said: "Keep out of this. You want to take away your mother's pleasure?" But this time I've got something on him. He's got three mistresses.'

'All my father ever does is pray to God,' said Number Five.

Noboru asked what he prayed for.

'Well, the family's safety, peace on earth, prosperity – stuff like that. He thinks we're a model home or

109

something. The bad part is he's even got my old lady thinking the same thing. The whole house is spick-and-span and everybody's supposed to be real honest and full of what he calls "the good". We even leave food out for the mice in the rafters so they won't have to sin by stealing. And you know what happens when dinner's over? Everybody hunches over and licks his plate clean so none of God's grace will be wasted.'

'Does your old man make you do that too?'

'He never *makes* you do anything. He starts doing all this crappy stuff himself and everybody else is sort of in the habit of copying him. . . . You're really lucky, Noboru. You should be thankful.'

Noboru was vexed at his immunity from the germs that infected the others, but at the same time he trembled at the fragility of his chance good fortune. Some providence he couldn't name had exempted him from evil. His purity was as brittle as a new moon. His innocence had sent an intricate net of feelers snaking towards the world, but when would they be snapped? When would the world lose its vastness and lace him in a straitjacket? That day, he knew, was not far away, and even now he could feel a lunatic courage swelling within him . . .

The Chief had turned away so as not to see Noboru's face. He was peering through a narrow gap in the crates at the convolutions of the smoke and clouds above the grey offing. He bit with small sharp shiny teeth at the red lining of his leather gloves.

Chapter 5

His mother's attitude changed. She became more affec-
tionate, devoted more time to looking after his needs.
Obviously this was the prelude to something he was going
to find difficult to accept.

One evening Noboru had said good night and was on
his way up to bed when Fusako climbed the stairs behind
him, calling, with a key ring in her hand: 'The key – I
almost forgot the key!' In this he sensed something unnatural. She always came upstairs with him to lock his
bedroom door and some nights she was gay and some
nights sullen, but this was the first time she had ever made
a speech about the key.

And then Ryuji, who was sitting in the living-room in a
maroon checked dressing-gown reading a book called *The
Reality of Merchandising*, looked up as though he had just
happened to overhear, and called his mother's name.

'Yes, Ryuji?' she said, turning on the stairs. Noboru
shuddered at the fawning sweetness in her voice.

'Don't you think it's time you stopped locking the boy's
door? After all, Noboru's not a child any more and he
knows what he should do and what he shouldn't. Isn't
that right, Noboru?'

The big voice from the living-room lumbered up the
stairs. In the darkness at the top, Noboru froze like a small
animal at bay, silent, his eyes gleaming. Fusako, who was
maintaining a gentleness as smooth as oil, didn't even
scold him for not answering.

'Well, I bet I know one happy young man around
here,' she said as she led him into his room. She checked

the textbooks on his desk against a timetable of classes for the next day and examined the points on his pencils. Ryuji had been helping him with maths every night and his marks had improved. Fusako's body, as she wandered round the room putting things in order, seemed so inordinately light and her movements so smooth that it was like watching an underwater dance. Finally she said good night and left. The long-familiar click of the lock never came.

As soon as he found himself alone, Noboru was uneasy. He had seen through the trick. But there was no comfort in that at all.

It was a trap – a rabbit trap. The grown-ups expected the captive animal's rage and the familiar odours of his lair to transform themselves into the resignation and tolerance of a creature who has confined himself. A hideously subtle trap: the rabbit, ensnared, was no longer a rabbit.

His uneasiness at being in the unlocked room made him shiver even after he had buttoned his pyjamas to the neck. They were beginning his education, a terrific, destructive education. Trying to force *maturity* on a thirteen-year-old boy. *Maturity* or, as the Chief would call it, *perversion*. Noboru's feverish brain was pursuing an impossibility: *Is there no way that I can remain in the room and at the same time be out in the hall locking the door?*

A few days later he came home from school to find Ryuji and Fusako dressed for the evening and was told that they were all going to see a film. It was a seventy-millimetre spectacular Noboru had been wanting to see and he was very pleased.

After the film they went to a restaurant in Chinatown and had dinner in a small private room upstairs. Noboru loved Chinese food; and he liked the dish-laden wooden tray which spun round and round in the centre of the table.

When all the food had been brought to the table, Ryuji signalled Fusako with his eyes. Apparently she was not prepared to face the moment sober : she had been sipping Chinese Lao-chu wine and already her eyes were a little red.

Noboru had never received such cordial treatment from the adults, nor had he ever seen them so ridiculously hesitant in his presence. It seemed to be some special adult ritual. He knew what they were going to say and it interested him very little. But he enjoyed watching them handle him from across the table as though he were a vulnerable, easily frightened, and all-innocent little bird – that was a real spectacle. They had laid the tender, down-ruffled little bird on a platter and appeared now to be pondering a way to eat out its heart without causing it distress.

Noboru didn't really object to the darling image of himself he knew Ryuji and his mother entertained in their imaginations. He would just have to be careful to look victimized.

'Noboru dear, I want you to listen carefully to what Mother is going to say because it's something very important,' Fusako began finally. 'You're going to have a dad again. Mr Tsukazaki is going to be your new father.'

As he listened Noboru succeeded in keeping his face a blank, and he was confident that he looked utterly bewildered. So far, so good. But he hadn't counted on the incredible nonsense that followed:

Part Two

'Your real dad was a wonderful man. You were eight years old when he passed away, so you must remember him and miss him very much. But I can't tell you how lonely Mother has been these past five years, and I know you've been lonely too. And you must have thought lots of times that both of us needed a new dad. I want you to understand, dear, how much I've wanted a strong, gentle, wonderful dad for both our sakes. And it's been all the harder because your father was such a fine, honest man. But you're a grown-up now, so I know you'll understand: how hard these five years have been, and how lonely, with just the two of us . . .' She fumbled an imported handkerchief out of her purse and began to cry: it was really too silly.

'Everything I've done has been for you, dear – everything. There isn't another man in this world as strong and as gentle and as wonderful in every way as Mr Tsukazaki. Noboru, I want you to call Mr Tsukazaki Dad now; we're going to be married early next month and we'll invite lots of friends and have a lovely party.'

Ryuji had averted his eyes from Noboru's impassive face and was engrossed in drinking, adding crystal sugar to the Lao-chu wine, stirring, tossing off the cup, and pouring himself another. He was afraid of seeming brazen to the boy.

Noboru knew that he was being feared as well as pitied, and the gentle threat had made him drunk: when he levelled the full iciness of his heart at the adults, a smile was playing at the corners of his mouth. It was hardly more than a wisp of a smile, the kind you see on the face of a schoolboy who has come to class unprepared but cocksure as a man leaping off a cliff; and yet, on the other side of the red formica table, Ryuji saw it out of the corner of

114

his eye and snatched it up. Again, a misunderstanding. The grin he flashed back was the same brand of exaggerated glee as his smile that day near the park when, to Noboru's intense disappointment and humiliation, he had appeared in a dripping-wet shirt.

'Fair enough. Then I won't call you Noboru any more. From now on, it's Son. What do you say, Son? Shake hands with Dad.' Ryuji placed one hard open hand on the table; Noboru struggled towards it as though he were paddling under water. No matter how he stretched, Ryuji's fingers seemed just beyond reach. At last their hands met, thick fingers grasped his own, and the hot, calloused handshake began. Noboru felt a whirlwind catch him up and spin him away towards the tepid, formless world he dreaded most ...

That night, as soon as Fusako had left his room and closed the door without locking it, Noboru's head began to swim. Hard heart ... hard heart: he tried repeating the words to himself, but that only made him want to hold the genuine article in his hand. Hard as an iron anchor ...

Before leaving the room, his mother had turned off the gas heater. Now heat and cold were mingled in a pocket of tepid air. If he could just brush his teeth, put on his pyjamas in a hurry, and jump into bed, he would be all right.

But an evasive languor made even removing his turtleneck sweater seem a wearisome task. Never had he waited so anxiously for his mother to reappear, to come back to his room, for example, to mention something she had forgotten to say. Nor had he ever felt such contempt for her.

He waited in the gradually mounting cold. And, weary

115

of waiting, he abandoned himself to an absurd fantasy. His mother had come back and she was shouting: *It was all a lie. I'm so sorry to have made a game out of fooling you. Will you forgive me? We are most certainly not going to get married. If we did a thing like that the world would turn to chaos: ten tankers would sink in the harbour, and a thousand trains would be derailed; the glass in the windows all over the city would shatter, and every lovely rose would turn black as coal.*

But she did not come back and finally Noboru contrived a situation in which her return would mean real trouble. He could no longer distinguish cause from effect; possibly this unreasonable yearning for his mother was due to a desire to wound her even if he had to share the pain.

The courage propelling him now was frightening: his hands began to tremble. He hadn't touched the dresser since the night Fusako had stopped locking his door. There was a reason: shortly after Ryuji's return on the morning of the thirtieth of December, he had observed them through the peephole and managed to watch the progression of merging shapes to its dazzling climax; but the danger in sneaking into the wall in broad daylight, with the door not even locked, had discouraged him from risking the adventure again.

But now he felt like invoking curses, and longed for a small revolution. If he were really a genius and the world mere emptiness, then why shouldn't he have the ability to prove it? He would have only to open a tiny crack in the glossy teacup of a world the adults believed in.

Noboru bolted to the dresser and seized the handle. Ordinarily he removed the drawer as quietly as possible but this time he wrenched it loose and dropped it to the floor. Then he stood and listened. Not a sound in response from anywhere in the house, no footsteps thudding up the stairs, nothing. The stillness was absolute but for the pounding in his chest.

Noboru looked at his watch. It was only ten o'clock. Then a strange plot took shape in his mind: he would do his homework inside the dresser. The irony was beautiful, and what better way to mock the meanness of their suspicions?

Taking a torch and some English word cards, he wriggled into the chest. A mysterious force would draw his mother to the room. She would find him in the chest and guess his purpose. Shame and rage would inflame her. She would haul him out of the dresser and slap his face; then he would show her the word cards and protest, with eyes as innocent as a lamb's: 'But what did I do wrong? I was only studying. It's easier to concentrate in a small space. . . .' He stopped imagining the episode and laughed out loud, gasping in the dusty air.

The moment he huddled inside the chest he was calm again. The trembling and the trepidation seemed almost funny now; he even had a feeling he would be able to study well. Not that it really mattered: this was the world's outer edge. So long as he was here, Noboru was in contact with the naked universe. No matter how far you ran, escape beyond this point was impossible.

Bending his arms in the cramped space, he began to read the cards by the light of the torch.

abandon
By now this word was an old acquaintance: he knew it well.
ability
Was that any different from *genius*?

Part Two

aboard

A ship again; he recalled the loudspeaker ringing across the deck that day when Ryuji sailed. And then the colossal, golden siren, like a proclamation of despair.

absence
absolute

He didn't even turn off the torch, sinking, before he knew it, into sleep.

It was close on midnight when Ryuji and Fusako went up to the bedroom. The announcement at dinner had relieved them of a great weight and they felt that a new phase was beginning.

But when it was time to go to bed, a strange shame stirred in Fusako. All evening she had discussed matters of importance, touched too lingeringly on the emotions of kinship, and now, in addition to a deep sense of quiet and relief, she felt embarrassed in the presence of something she couldn't name, something unaccountably sacred.

Choosing a black négligée she knew Ryuji liked Fusako got into bed and, disregarding for the first time Ryuji's preference for a brightly lit room, asked him to turn out all the lights. He embraced her in the dark.

When it was done Fusako said: 'I thought I wouldn't feel embarrassed if all the lights were out, but it was just the opposite. The darkness becomes a huge eye and you feel as if you're being watched the whole time.'

Ryuji laughed at her nervousness and glanced around the room. The curtains on the windows shut out all light from the street. The gas heater burning in one corner gave off a pale reflection of bluish light. It was just like the night sky above a small distant city. The frail lustre of the brass bedposts trembled in the darkness.

Then Ryuji's eye fell on the wainscot along the wall adjoining the next room. From one spot on the ornately carved wooden border, light was trickling into the room.

'I wonder what that is,' he mused aloud. 'Do you think Noboru's still up? You know, this place is getting pretty run-down. I'd better seal that up in the morning.'

Like a snake coiling for the strike, Fusako lifted her bare white neck from the bed and peered through the darkness at the point of light. She comprehended with terrific speed. One movement carried her out of bed and into a dressing-gown; then she bolted from the room without a word. Ryuji called after her but there was no answer.

He heard Noboru's door open. Silence. A muffled sound that might have been Fusako crying; Ryuji slid out of bed. He paced the floor in the darkness trying to decide whether he should go straight in or wait, and finally, sitting down on the couch near the window, lit a cigarette.

Noboru started from sleep as something ferociously strong hauled him out of the dresser by the seat of his pants. For a minute, he didn't realize what had happened. His mother's slender, supple hands were falling on his nose, lips and mouth, and he couldn't keep his eyes open. It was the first time she had ever laid hands on him.

He lay almost prostrate on the floor, one of his legs thrust into a tangle of shirts and underwear scattered when they had stumbled over the drawer. He hadn't imagined his mother could muster such terrific strength.

Finally he managed to look up at the panting figure glaring down at him.

Part Two

The skirts of her dark-blue robe were wide open, the fleshy swells of her lower body looked grotesquely massive and threatening. Soaring high above the gradually tapering trunk was her face, gasping, grief-stricken, turned horribly old in an instant and drenched in tears. The bulb in the distant ceiling wreathed her bedraggled hair with a lunatic halo.

All this Noboru took in at a glance and at the back of his icy brain a memory stirred: it was as if he had participated in this same moment a long time ago. This, beyond a doubt, was the punishment scene he had watched so often in his dreams.

His mother began to sob and, still glaring down at him through her tears, she screamed in tones he could scarcely understand: 'It's humiliating – it's just so humiliating! My own son, a filthy, disgusting thing like that – I could die this very minute! Oh, Noboru, how could you have done this to me!'

To his surprise, Noboru discovered that he had lost all desire to protest that he had been studying English. Not that this would have made any difference now. Obviously, his mother was not mistaken; and she had brushed against 'reality', a thing she dreaded worse than leeches. In one sense, that made them more nearly equal now than they had ever been: it was almost empathy. Pressing his palms to his reddened, burning cheeks, Noboru resolved to watch carefully how a person drawn so near could retreat in one fleeting instant to an unattainable distance. Clearly it was not the discovery of reality itself that had spawned her indignation and her grief: Noboru knew that his mother's shame and despair derived from a kind of prejudice. She had been quick to interpret the reality, and inasmuch as her banal interpretation was the cause

120

of all her agitation, no clever excuse from him would serve any purpose.

'I'm afraid this is more than I can handle,' Fusako said finally, her voice ominously quiet. 'A frightening child like this is too much for me. . . . You just wait a minute! I'm going to see that Father punishes you so that you won't dare think of this kind of thing again.' It was clear that Fusako expected her threat to make Noboru cry and apologize.

But then her resolution faltered; for the first time, she considered dealing with the problem later. If she could get Noboru to apologize before Ryuji came into the room, she would be able to hide the details from him and save her pride as a mother. In that case the tears and the apology would have to come quickly; but she couldn't suggest that mother and son conspire to resolve the problem, for she had threatened that the father would punish him. She could only wait in silence.

But Noboru didn't say a word. He was interested only in the ultimate destination of the great engine now in motion. In that dark hole inside the chest he had stood at the outermost limit of his world, at the edge of the seas and the deserts. And because all things took life there, because he was to be punished for having been there, he could not return to the tepid towns of men, nor lower his face to their tear-moistened lawns. On the oath he had sworn to that beautiful pinnacle of humanity swathed in the roar of that siren, sworn to the gleaming representatives of order he had seen through the peephole that summer night, he could never turn back again.

The door opened tentatively and Ryuji peeped into the room.

Fusako saw that she and her son had lost an opportunity,

and she grew angry again. Either Ryuji should have stayed away altogether or he should have come in with her at the beginning.

Irritated by Ryuji's clumsy entrance and struggling to sort out her feelings, Fusako became more furious with Noboru than ever.

'Would you mind telling me what's going on here?' Ryuji said as he came into the room.

'I want you to punish him, Father. If this child isn't beaten within an inch of his life the evil in him will keep getting worse. He was spying on us through a hole in the chest there.'

'Is that right, Son?' There was no anger in Ryuji's voice.

Still sprawled on the floor, his legs flung out in front of him, Noboru nodded.

'I see. . . . Well, I suppose the idea just sort of hit you all of a sudden and you tried it tonight?'

Noboru shook his head emphatically.

'Oh? Then you've done the same thing maybe once or twice before?'

Again Noboru shook his head.

'Then this has been going on from the very beginning?'

Seeing the boy nod, Fusako and Ryuji exchanged involuntary glances. Noboru had a pleasant vision of the lightning in the adults' gaze illuminating the life on shore that Ryuji dreamed about and Fusako's respectable household as they crashed noisily into rubble – but in his excitement he had given too free a rein to his imagination. He had been expecting an impassioned reaction.

'I see,' was all Ryuji said. His hands were stuffed into the pockets of his dressing-gown. The hairy legs protruding below the robe were directly in front of Noboru's face.

Now Ryuji was obliged to reach a father's decision, the first decision about shore life he had ever been forced to make. But his memory of the sea's fury was tempering his critical notions of land and the landsman with inordinate mildness, and his instinctive approach to problems was therefore thwarted. To beat the boy would be easy enough, but a difficult future awaited him. He would have to receive their love with dignity, to deliver them from daily dilemmas, to balance daily accounts; he was expected in some vague, general way to comprehend the incomprehensible feelings of the mother and the child and to become an infallible teacher, perceiving the causes of a situation even as unconscionable as this one; he was dealing here with no ocean squall but the gentle breeze that blows ceaselessly over the land.

Though Ryuji didn't realize it, the distant influence of the sea was at work on him again: he was unable to distinguish the most exalted feelings from the meanest, and suspected that vitally important things did not occur on land. No matter how hard he tried to reach a realistic decision, shore matters remained suffused with the hues of fantasy.

In the first place, it would be a mistake to interpret literally Fusako's plea that he beat Noboru. Sooner or later, he knew, she would come to feel grateful for his leniency. Besides, he found himself believing in the paternal instinct. As he hurried to banish from his mind merely dutiful concern for this reticent, precocious, bothersome child, this boy whom he didn't really love, Ryuji managed to convince himself that he was brimming with genuine fatherly affection. It seemed to him, moreover, that he was discovering the emotion for the first time, and he was surprised at the unpredictability of his affections.

123

Part Two

'I see,' he said again, lowering himself slowly to the floor and crossing his legs.

'You sit down too, Mother. I've been thinking, and it seems to me that Noboru isn't the only one to blame for what's happened. When I came into this house, Son, your life changed too. Not that it was wrong for me to come, but your life *did* change, and it's natural for a boy in junior high school to feel curious about changes in his life. What you did was wrong, there's no question about that, but from now on I want you to direct that curiosity towards your school work, do you understand?

'You have nothing to say about what you saw. And nothing to ask. You're not a child any more and some day we'll be able to laugh together and talk about what's happened here as three adults. Mother, I want you to calm down too. We're going to forget about the past and face the future happily, hand in hand. I'll seal that hole up in the morning and then we can all forget this whole unpleasant evening. Right? What you do say, Noboru?'

Noboru listened, feeling as though he were about to suffocate. *Can this man be saying things like that? This splendid hero who once shone so brightly?*

Every word burned like fire. He wanted to scream, as his mother had screamed: *How can you do this to me?* The sailor was saying things he was never meant to say. Ignoble things in wheedling, honeyed tones, foul words not meant to issue from his lips until Doomsday, words such as men mutter in stinking lairs. And he was speaking proudly, for he believed in himself, was satisfied with the role of father he had stepped forward to accept.

He is satisfied. Noboru felt nauseated. Tomorrow Ryuji's slavish hands, the hands of a father pottering over carpentry of a Sunday afternoon, would close for ever the narrow access to that unearthly brilliance which he himself had once revealed.

'Right? What do you say, Son?' Ryuji concluded, clapping a hand on Noboru's shoulder. He tried to shake free and couldn't. He was thinking that the Chief had been right: there were worse things than being beaten.

Chapter 6

Noboru asked the Chief to call an emergency meeting: on their way home from school, the boys assembled at the swimming pool next to the foreign cemetery.

Climbing down a horse's back of a hill thick with giant oaks was one way to reach the pool. Half-way down they stopped and gazed through the evergreen trees at the cemetery below: quartz sparkled in the winter light.

From this point on the hill, the tombstones and stone crosses ranged in long terraced rows were all facing away from them. The inky green of sago palm bloomed among the graves; greenhouse flower cuttings laid in the shadows of stone crosses brightened the lawn with unseasonable reds and greens.

Above the rooftops in the valley loomed the Marine Tower, the foreigners' graves lay to the right, and in a smaller valley to the left the pool waited. In the off season, the tiered seats there made an excellent meeting-place.

Tripping over bared tree roots which swelled like tumid black blood vessels across the face of the slope, the boys scrambled down the hill and broke on to the withered grass path that led into the evergreens surrounding the pool. The pool was drained, and very quiet. The blue

125

paint on the bottom was chipping; dry leaves had piled up in the corners. The blue steel ladder stopped far short of the bottom. Banking into the west now, the sun was hidden behind the cliffs which enclosed the valley like folding screens: dusk had come already to the bottom of the pool.

Noboru trailed along behind the others; he could still see in his mind the backs of all those endless foreign graves – graves and crosses all turned away from him. Then what would this outlandish place be called?

They sat in a diamond pattern on the blackened concrete seats. Noboru took out of his briefcase a slim notebook and handed it to the Chief without a word. Inked on the cover in venomous red was 'Charges against Ryuji Tsukazaki'.

Craning their necks to see, the boys read the text together. It was an excerpt from Noboru's diary; the dresser-drawer incident of the night before brought the number of entries to eighteen.

'This is terrible,' the Chief wailed. 'This last one alone is worth about thirty-five points. And the total – let's see – even if you go easy and call this first charge five points, they get worse the closer they get to the end: I'm afraid the total's way over a hundred and fifty. I didn't realize it was quite this bad. We're going to have to do something about this.'

As he listened to the Chief, Noboru began to tremble. Finally he asked: 'Is there any chance of saving him?'

'None at all. It's too bad, though.'

A long silence followed. This the Chief interpreted as indicating a lack of courage and he began to speak again, twisting between his fingers the tough vein of a dried leaf he had pulverized: 'All six of us are geniuses. And the

126

world, as you know, is empty. I know I've said this before, but have you ever thought about it carefully? Because to assume for those reasons that we are permitted to do anything we want is sloppy thinking. As a matter of fact, we are the ones who do the permitting. Teachers, schools, fathers, society – we permit all those garbage heaps. And not because we're powerless either. Permitting is our special privilege and if we felt any pity at all we wouldn't be ruthless enough to permit this. What it amounts to is that we are constantly permitting unpermissible things. There are only a very few really permissible things: like the sea, for example –'

'And ships,' Noboru added.

'Right – anyway, very few. And if they conspire against us, it's just as if your own dog were to bite a hunk out of your hand. It's a direct insult to our special privilege.'

'We've never done anything about it before,' interrupted Number One.

'That doesn't mean we're never going to,' the Chief answered adroitly, his voice benign. 'But getting back to Ryuji Tsukazaki,' he continued, 'he's never meant much to the group as a whole, but for Number Three he was a person of considerable importance. At least, he's credited with having shown Number Three some luminous evidence of the internal order of life I've mentioned so often. But then he betrayed Number Three. He became the worst thing on the face of this earth, a father. And something has to be done. It would have been much better if he'd just stayed the useless sailor he started out by being.

'As I've said before, life consists of simple symbols and decisions. Ryuji may not have known it, but he was one of those symbols. At least, according to Number Three's testimony it *seems* that he was.

127

Part Two

'I'm sure you all know where our duty lies. When a gear slips out of place it's our job to force it back into position. If we don't, order will turn to chaos. We all know that the world is empty and that the important thing, the only thing, is to try to maintain order in that emptiness. And so we are guards, and more than that, because we also have executive power to ensure that order is maintained.'

The Chief stated the conclusion simply: 'We'll have to pass sentence. In the long run it's for his own good. Number Three! Do you remember that day on the pier when I said there was only one way to make him a hero again, and that soon I'd be able to tell you what it was?'

'I remember,' Noboru answered, trying to keep his legs from trembling.

'Well, the time has come.'

The other boys sought each other's faces, then sat motionless and silent. They understood the grave importance of what the Chief was about to say.

They gazed into the empty, dusk-shadowed pool. White lines were painted on the chipped blue bottom. The dry leaves in the corners had sifted in like dust.

At that moment, the pool was enormously deep. Deeper and deeper as watery blue darkness seeped up from the bottom. The knowledge, so certain it was sensuous, that nothing was there to support the body if one plunged in generated around the empty pool an unremitting tension. Gone now was the soft summer water that received the swimmer's body and bore him lightly afloat, but the pool, like a monument to summer and to water, had endured, and it was dangerous, lethal.

The blue steel ladder crept over the edge and down into

the pool and, still far from the bottom, stopped. Nothing there to support a body, nothing at all!

'Classes are over at two tomorrow; we can have him meet us here and then take him out to our dry dock at Sugita. Number Three, it's up to you to lure him down here somehow.

'I'm going to give the rest of you instructions now. Please remember what you're supposed to bring. I'll take care of the sleeping pills and the scalpel myself. We won't be able to handle a powerful man like that unless we knock him out first. Adults are supposed to take one to three tablets of that German stuff we've got at home, so he should go out like a light if we give him about seven. I'll make powder out of the tablets so they'll dissolve quicker in tea.

'Number One, you're to bring some six-foot lengths of strong hemp rope; you'd better have – let's see – one, two, three, four – make it five lengths just to be sure. Number Two, you prepare a thermos of hot tea and hide it in your briefcase. Since Number Three has the job of getting him down here, he doesn't have to bring any-thing. We'll need sugar and spoons, and paper cups for us and a dark-coloured plastic cup for him – that'll be your job, Number Four. Number Five, you get some cloth for a blindfold and a towel we can use for a gag.

'You can each bring any kind of cutting tool you like – knives, saws, whatever you prefer.

'We've already practised the essentials on a cat and this'll be the same, so there's nothing to worry about. The job's a little bigger this time, that's all – and it may stink a little worse.'

The boys sat dumb as stones and stared into the empty pool.

Part Two

'Are you scared, Number One?' Number One managed a slight shake of his head.

'How about you, Number Two?' As though suddenly cold, the boy stuffed his hands into his overcoat pockets.

'What's wrong, Number Three?' Noboru was gasping for breath, his mouth utterly dry as if stuffed with straw: he couldn't answer.

'That's what I was afraid of. You're all great talkers, but when the chips are down you haven't got one thimbleful of nerve. Well, maybe this will make you feel better; I brought it along just in case.' The Chief produced from his briefcase an ochre law-book and deftly flipped it open to the page he wanted.

'I want all of you to listen carefully: "Penal Code, Article Fourteen,"' he read. *"'Acts of juveniles less than fourteen years of age are not punishable by law."* I'll read it again as loud as I can: *"Acts of juveniles less than fourteen years of age are not punishable by law."'*

The Chief had the others pass the book around while he continued: 'You might say that our fathers and the fictitious society they believe in passed this law for our benefit. And I think we should be grateful to them. This law is the adults' way of expressing the high hopes they have for us. But it also represents all the dreams they've never been able to make come true. They've assumed just because they've roped themselves so tight they can't even budge that we must be helpless too; they've been careless enough to allow us here, and only here, a glimpse of blue sky and absolute freedom.

'This law they've written is a kind of nursery tale, a pretty deadly nursery tale, I'd say. And in a way it's understandable. After all, up to now we *have* been nursery kids, adorable, defenceless, innocent kids.

'But three of us here will be fourteen next month – myself, Number One, and you, Number Three. And you other three will be fourteen in March. Just think about it a minute. This is our last chance!'

The Chief scrutinized their faces and saw tension easing out of their cheeks, fear dwindling away. Awakening for the first time to society's genial benevolence, the boys felt secure in the knowledge that their enemies were actually their protectors.

Noboru looked up at the sky. Afternoon blue was fading into the shifting greys of dusk. Suppose Ryuji tried at the height of his heroic death throes to look up at this hallowed sky? It seemed a shame to blindfold him.

'This is our last chance,' the Chief repeated. 'If we don't act now we will never again be able to obey freedom's supreme command, to perform the deed essential to filling the emptiness of the world, unless we are prepared to sacrifice our lives. And you can see that it's absurd for the executioners to risk their own lives. If we don't act now we'll never be able to steal again, or murder, or do any of the things that testify to a man's freedom. We'll end up puking flattery and gossip, trembling our days away in submission and compromise and fear, worrying about what the neighbours are doing, living like squealing mice. And some day we'll get married, and have kids, and finally we'll become fathers, the vilest things on earth!

'We must have blood! Human blood! If we don't get it this empty world will go pale and shrivel up. We must drain that sailor's fresh lifeblood and transfuse it to the dying universe, the dying sky, the dying forests, and the drawn, dying land.

'Now! The time is now! In another month they'll have

131

finished clearing the land around our dry dock and then the place will fill up with people. Besides, we're almost fourteen.'

The Chief glanced through a black frame of evergreen branches at the watery grey sky and observed: 'Looks like tomorrow will be a nice day.'

Chapter 7

On the morning of the twenty-second, Fusako went with Ryuji to the Town Hall to ask the Mayor of Yokohama if he would be toastmaster at their wedding dinner. He said he would be honoured. On the way back, they stopped at a department store and ordered engraved wedding announcements. Bookings for the reception had already been made at the New Grand Hotel. After an early lunch downtown, they returned to Rex.

Just after one, Ryuji left the shop to keep an appointment he had mentioned earlier in the day. A high-school classmate who was now a First Officer had docked that morning at Takashima Pier and was free to meet him only in the early afternoon. And Ryuji didn't want to appear in an expensive English suit. He didn't like the idea of flaunting his new circumstances in front of an old friend; at least not until after the wedding. He would stop at the house on his way to the dock and change into his old seaman's clothes.

'Are you sure I don't have to worry that you'll get on that ship and disappear?' Fusako teased as she accompanied him to the door.

Noboru, pretending to need help with homework, had

132

summoned Ryuji conspiratorially to his room the night before and entrusted him with a mission which he was discharging faithfully:

'Dad, all the fellows are looking forward to hearing some of your sea stories tomorrow afternoon. We're going to meet on that hill above the pool when school's over at two. Everybody's been wanting to meet you and I promised you'd come. You will, won't you? And tell them some of your adventures? And would you wear your sailor clothes like you used to, and your sailor cap? Only it's got to be a secret from Mum. You could tell her you're going to meet an old friend or something and get off work early.'

This was the first son-to-father favour Noboru had ever asked and Ryuji was determined not to betray the boy's trust. It was a father's duty. Even if the truth came out later it would only mean having a good laugh together, so he had fabricated a plausible story and left the shop early.

Ryuji was sitting on the roots of a giant oak near the top of the hill when the boys appeared just after two. One of them, a boy with crescent eyebrows and red lips who seemed particularly bright, thanked him politely for having come, and then suggested that a more suitable spot for his talk would be what he called their dry dock. Assuming they were heading somewhere near the harbour, Ryuji agreed to go.

It was a mild midwinter afternoon. The shade was chilly, but in the sun, which reached them through a wispy layer of cloud, they didn't need their overcoats. Ryuji was wearing his grey turtleneck sweater and carried his pea-jacket over his arm; the six boys, each with a brief-case, anticked around him as he walked along, now surging ahead, now falling behind. For this generation, they were smallish boys: the scene reminded Ryuji of six tug-boats labouring ineffectively to tow a freighter out to sea. He didn't notice that their frolicking had a kind of frenzied uneasiness.

The boy with the crescent eyebrows informed him they were going to take a tram. Ryuji was surprised, but made no objection: he understood that the setting for a story was important to boys of this age. No one made any move to get off until the last stop at Sugita, which was far south of the city.

'Say, where are you fellows taking me?' he asked repeatedly, as though amused. He had determined to spend a day with the boys and it wouldn't do to appear annoyed, no matter what happened.

Though careful not to draw attention to the fact, he was observing Noboru constantly. As the boy mingled happily with his friends, Ryuji saw the piercing look of cross-examination go out of his eyes for the first time. It was like watching motes of dust dance into colour in the winter light streaming through the tram window: boundaries between Noboru and the others became blurred, and he confused them. That had hardly seemed possible, not with a boy so different from everyone else, a lonely boy with a peculiar habit of eyeing adults furtively. And it proved that Ryuji had been right to take half a day off in order to amuse Noboru and his friends. Right, he knew, in terms of a father's moral obligation. Most books and magazines would agree. Noboru had approached voluntarily and offered in this excursion a providential opportunity to cement their relationships. It was a chance for a father and son originally strangers to forge a bond of deep and tender trust stronger than mere blood ties could ever be. And since Ryuji could very well

134

have become a father when he was twenty, there was nothing out of the ordinary about Noboru's age.

As soon as they were off the tram, the boys began tugging Ryuji towards a road which wound into the hills. 'Hey, wait a minute,' he protested. 'I never heard of a dry dock in the mountains!'

'No? But in Tokyo the subway runs up above your head!'

'I can see I'm no match for you fellows.' Ryuji winced, and the boys howled, thoroughly pleased with themselves.

The road skirted the ridge of Aoto Hill and entered Kanazawa Ward. They passed an electric power plant with its web of power lines and gnarled porcelain insulators thrown up against the winter sky, then entered Tomioka Tunnel. Emerging on the other side, they saw glinting along the ridge to the right the tracks of the Tokyo-Yokohama express; bright, new housing sites covered the slope to the left.

'Almost there now. We go up between those sites. All this used to be an American Army installation.' The boy who seemed to be their leader tossed the explanation over one shoulder and stepped ahead; his manner and language, in a matter of minutes, had become brusque.

Work on the sites had been completed; there were even stone boundary fences and the skeletons of more than a few houses. Surrounding Ryuji, the six boys marched straight up the road that ran between the sites. Near the top of the hill, the road disappeared abruptly and a terrace of uncultivated fields began. It was like clever sleight of hand: a man standing at the bottom of the hill would never guess that the straight, well-graded road gave way at this point on the slope to a grassy wilderness.

There wasn't a soul in sight. The heavy droning of

135

bulldozers echoed from the other side of the hill. Sounds of motor traffic ascended from the tunnel road far below. Except for the echoes of engine noise, the vast landscape was empty and the sounds themselves only heightened the bright desolation.

Here and there wooden stakes thrust up from the grass; they were beginning to rot. A footpath buried under fallen leaves skirted the ridge of the hill. They crossed the withered field. Just off to the right, a rusty water tank surrounded by a tangle of barbed wire lay half buried in the ground; bolted lopsidedly to the tank was a sheet of rusting tin lettered in English. Ryuji stopped and read the notice:

<blockquote>
U.S. Forces Installation
Unauthorized Entry Prohibited and Punishable
under Japanese Law
</blockquote>

'What's "punishable" mean?' the leader asked. There was something about the boy Ryuji didn't like. The flicker of light in his eye when he asked the question suggested that he knew the answer perfectly well. Ryuji forced himself to explain politely.

'Oh – but this isn't army property any more, so I guess we can do whatever we want. Look!' Even as he spoke the boy appeared to have forgotten the subject, as though it were a balloon he had abandoned to the sky.

'Here's the top.'

Ryuji stepped to the summit and gazed at the panorama stretching below. 'You've got yourselves quite a place here.'

The hill overlooked Tokyo Bay. Away to the left, bulldozers were cutting a red-loam slope into the side of a cliff and dump trucks were hauling the earth away.

Distance dwarfed the trucks but the roar of their engines battered endless waves into the choppy air. Farther down in the valley were the grey roofs of an industrial laboratory and an aircraft factory; in the concrete garden in front of the central offices, one small pine was bathed in sun.

Around the factory curled an isolated country village. The thin winter sunlight accentuated the highs and lows in the rows of rooftops and the files of shadow cast by countless ridgepoles. The objects glinting like seashells through the thin smoke that covered the valley were car windows.

As it neared the sea, the landscape appeared to fold in on itself and assumed a special quality of rust, and sadness, and clutter. Beyond a tangle of rusted machinery discarded on the beach, a vermilion crane swung in wobbly arcs, and, beyond the crane, there was the sea, the piled white of stone breakwaters and, at the edge of the reclaimed foreshore, a green dredger smoking blackly.

The sea made Ryuji feel that he had been away from it a long, long time. Fusako's bedroom overlooked the harbour but he never went near the window any more. The water, with spring still far away, was Prussian blue except where the shadow of one pearly cloud turned it pale, chilly white. The rest of the mid-afternoon sky was cloudless, a bleached, monotone blue fading where it neared the horizon.

The sea spread from the dirtied shore towards the offing like a huge ochre net. There were no ships close in to shore; several freighters were moving across the offing, small vessels which, even at this distance, were obviously antique.

'The ship I was on was no little tug like that.'

'I'll say – the *Rakuyo* had a displacement of ten

137

thousand tons,' Noboru affirmed. He had spoken hardly a word all afternoon.

'C'mon, let's go,' the leader urged, tugging at Ryuji's sleeve. Descending the footpath a short distance, they came to a segment of land miraculously untouched by the surrounding devastation, a vestige of the mountain-top as it must once have been. The clearing, on one of a twisting series of slopes sheltered from the east wind by a line of oaks and protected to the west by the heavily wooded hilltop, merged into a neglected field of winter rye. Withered vines snaked through the undergrowth round the path; sitting at the tip of one was a shrivelled, blood-red gourd. Sunlight from the western sky was thwarted the moment it descended here: a few pale beams flickered over the tips of dead leaves.

Ryuji, though he remembered having done similar things in his own youth, marvelled at a young boy's unique ability to discover this sort of hiding-place and make it his own.

'Which one of you fellows found this place?'

'I did. But I live right over in Sugita. I pass by here lots of times on the way to school. I found it and showed the others.'

'And where's this dry dock of yours?'

'Over here.' The leader was standing in front of a small cave shadowed by the hilltop, smiling as he pointed at the entrance.

To Ryuji the smile seemed as brittle as fine glass crystal and very dangerous. He couldn't say why he thought so. With the adroitness of a minnow slipping through a net, the boy shifted his gaze away from Ryuji's face and continued the explanation.

'This is our dry dock. A dry dock on top of a mountain.

We repair run-down ships here, dismantle them first and then rebuild them from the ground up.'

'Is that right? . . . Must be quite a job hauling a ship way up here.'

'It's easy – nothing to it,' the boy said, and the too pretty smile lit his face again.

They sat down on the faintly green, as though grass-stained, ground in front of the cave. It was very cold in the shade and the sea breeze spanked their faces. Ryuji hunched into his pea-jacket and crossed his legs. He had just settled himself when the bulldozers began their din again.

'Well, have any of you fellows ever been aboard a really big ship?' he ventured, with forced cheeriness.

They glanced around at each other, but no one answered.

'You talk about life at sea,' he began again, facing his stolid audience, 'you have to begin with getting seasick. Any sailor's been through it one time or another. And I've known men to chuck up the sponge after one cruise, they've had such a hell of a time with it. The larger the ship is, the more mixture of rolling and pitching you get; and there are some special smells too, like paint and oil and food cooking in the galley . . .'

When he saw they weren't interested in seasickness, he tried a song for lack of anything else. 'Did you fellows ever hear this song?

'The whistle wails and streamers tear,
Our ship slips away from the pier.
Now the sea's my home, I decided that.
But even I must shed a tear
As I wave, boys, as I wave so sad
At the harbour town where my heart was glad.'

Part Two

The boys nudged each other and giggled, and finally burst out laughing. Noboru was embarrassed to death. He stood up abruptly and, plucking Ryuji's cap from his head, turned his back on the others and began to toy with it.

The anchor at the centre of the large, tear-shaped emblem was girded with chains of gold thread and wreathed in laurel branches embroidered in gold and hung with silver berries. Above and below the emblem, hawsers of gold braid were looped in slack coils. The peak was austere; reflecting the afternoon sun, it shone with a mournful lustre.

Once, at sunset on a summer day, this marvellous cap had receded over a dazzling sea, becoming a glittering emblem of farewell and the unknown. This very cap, receding until it was free of the high injunctions of existence, had become an exalted firebrand lighting the way to eternity!

'My first voyage was on a freighter bound for Hong Kong. . . .' As he began to talk about his career, Ryuji felt the boys growing more attentive. He told them of his experiences on that first voyage, the failures, the confusion, the longing, and the melancholy. Then he started on anecdotes collected on voyages around the world: waiting in Suez harbour for clearance through the canal when someone discovered that one of the hawsers had been stolen; the watchman in Alexandria who spoke Japanese and conspired with merchants on the pier to foist various vulgar items on the crew (details of these Ryuji withheld as being unsuitable material for the classroom); the unimaginable difficulty of taking on coal at Newcastle in Australia and then readying the ship for the next load before they reached Sydney, a journey logged in a single watch; encountering off the coast of South America a United Fruit transport vessel and the sea air suddenly redolent of the tropical fruit brimming in the hatches...

Half-way through his story, Ryuji happened to glance up and saw the leader slipping on a pair of long latex gloves. Tensing his fingers, the boy crossed them nervously again and again as if to glue the cold rubber to his flesh.

Ryuji ignored him. A bright student bored with class was acting on a whim – a meaningless display. Besides, the more he talked, the more insistently recollection was prodding him; turning, he gazed at the thin line of con-densed blue which was the sea.

Trailing black smoke, a small ship was teetering on the horizon. He could have been aboard that ship himself. Gradually, as he talked to the boys, Ryuji had come to understand himself as Noboru imagined him.

I could have been a man sailing away for ever. He had been fed up with it all, glutted, and yet now, slowly, he was awakening again to the immensity of what he had abandoned.

The dark passions of the tides, the shriek of a tidal wave, the avalanching break of surf upon a shoal . . . an unknown glory calling for him endlessly from the dark offing, glory merged in death and in a woman, glory to fashion of his destiny something special, something rare. At twenty he had been passionately certain: in the depths of the world's darkness was a point of light which had been provided for him alone and would draw near some day to irradiate him and no other.

Whenever he dreamed of them, glory and death and woman were consubstantial. Yet when the woman had been attained, the other two withdrew beyond the offing and ceased their mournful wailing of his name. The things he had rejected were now rejecting him.

Not that the blast furnace of a world had ever been his to call his own, but at one time he had felt the sun fasten on his flank, beneath the tropical palms he missed so much, and gnaw his flesh with sharp, hot teeth. Now only embers remained. Now began a peaceful life, a life bereft of motion.

Now perilous death had rejected him. And glory, no doubt of that. And the retching drunkenness of his own feelings. The piercing grief, the radiant farewells. The call of the Grand Cause, another name for the tropical sun, and the women's gallant tears, and the dark longing, and the sweet heavy power propelling him towards the pinnacle of manliness – now all this was done, finished.

'Want some tea?' The leader's high, clear voice rang out behind him.

'Okay . . .' Ryuji mused on without even turning his head. He recalled the shapes of islands he had visited. Makatea in the South Pacific and New Caledonia. The West Indies: seething with languor and melancholy, teeming with condor and parrots and, everywhere you looked, palms. Emperor palms. Wine palms. Surging out of the splendour of the sea, death had swept down on him like a stormy bank of clouds. A vision of death now eternally beyond his reach, majestic, acclaimed, heroic death unfurled its rapture across his brain. And if the world had been provided for just this radiant death, then why shouldn't the world also perish for it?

Waves, as tepid as blood, inside an atoll. The tropical sun blaring across the sky like the call of a brass trumpet. The many-coloured sea. Sharks . . .

Winter

Another step or two and Ryuji would have begun to have regrets.

'Here's your tea,' Noboru offered from behind him, thrusting a dark-brown plastic cup near Ryuji's cheek. Absently, Ryuji took it. He noticed Noboru's hand trembling slightly, probably from the cold.

Still immersed in his dream, he drank down the tepid tea. It tasted bitter. Glory, as anyone knows, is bitter stuff.